Contents

Story I

Gladys the Blue Whale

This is the story of a large whale called Gladys. Poor Gladys was very lonely because she had no friends. Everyone laughed at her because she was blue!

You all know that whales are usually grey, but Gladys was blue. Her tail was blue, her tummy was blue, her back was blue, but her teeth were white, a beautiful pearly white. She lived all alone in the lagoon. No-one came near her. She could see all the other fishes and turtles playing outside her coral reef.

The turtles gave each other piggy-backs and the dolphins did clever tricks with bits of rubbish they found floating about. Even the shoals of brilliant-coloured fish seemed to be moving rainbows. Poor Gladys watched, sadly wishing she was grey, or even red, anything but blue! Blue was such a silly colour to be.

Well, one day, Gladys decided to go outside her lagoon. She hadn't been outside for years. The sun was coming up as Gladys swam out through the gap in the coral reef. As she swam, she heard the turtles calling to each other, but she took no notice. The rainbow fish glided past, laughing and whispering to each other. Even the seaweed seemed to be talking about her.

"I'll show them. One day I will be famous and then they will want to talk to me," thought Gladys. Off she went with the sun warming her back as she surfaced. All around her were bits of rubbish and oil. "Oh how horrible," she said to herself, "I hope that does not get into my lagoon. I wonder where it has come from?" She swam on silently, deep in thought, when suddenly she bumped into a large, drifting piece of wood. BUMP! Her eyes filled with flashing lights and it took a few minutes to steady herself. She blinked, then looked closely at the piece of wood. Clinging to it was a small child! His eyes were full of fear and he was wearing torn clothes.

"Oh dear me, a small boy and he is all alone. He doesn't look very well. I wonder where his mummy and daddy are?" wondered Gladys.

She swam around the piece of wood, looking everywhere. There was no-one about, so she swam back to the piece of wood and saw the small boy looking at her with his big, brown eyes. She could see he was very frightened. She flapped her flipper in the water to show him she was his friend, but he started to cry. "What shall I do?" thought Gladys. "He is too little to be alone, and anyway, he is not a fish so he cannot live in the sea."

Gladys did a quick flip with her tail which made the piece of wood move gently. Suddenly she had an idea! "If I push the piece of wood towards the beach, someone will find it and then he will be safe. Yes, that is what I will do." She swam towards the piece of wood, nudged it gently and it started to move slowly in front of her. The little boy clung tightly onto it, watching Gladys. Again and again she flipped her flipper, nudging the wood towards the beach. It seemed as if she was pushing it for miles, but suddenly her eyes caught sight of some yellow sand – the beach. "Yes, that is the place," she thought. She looked across to the small boy and was sure she almost saw a smile. She winked her little eye to show she was happy for him.

Gladys continued pushing the piece of wood until she heard a grating sound and it would not go any further. A final push and a big wave put it right up onto the beach.

She was so pleased and so happy – for once in her life she had been *important* and her blue colour had not mattered. She had actually saved a little boy from certain death! Now she would be famous and maybe the other creatures would talk to her? As she flipped over onto her back, she looked out towards the beach. The little boy was surrounded by a crowd of people. Two of these people were holding him very close and he was pointing out to sea and waving. "Oh, he loves me, he loves me!" cried Gladys to herself. "Hooray!"

Her back arched into another flip, then she rolled over onto her side and waved her flipper. "Bye bye little boy, take care of yourself." Slowly she swam back to the lagoon, one very happy blue whale.....

But, as she got near to the lagoon, she saw the dolphins, the turtles and the rainbow fish all watching her. She held her head high and glided majestically towards her lagoon. Suddenly she heard clapping and cheering!

"Well done Gladys!" "You were very clever." "How brave you were." All the creatures were calling out to her.

"WOW! Thank you," said Gladys as she smiled at them all.

"Would you like to come and play with us?" asked the dolphins.

"Will you play with us too?" said the turtles.

"And us, and us!" sang the rainbow fish.

"Oh yes *please*! I would love to!" smiled Gladys and off she went, surrounded by her new friends. She was never lonely again. No-one laughed at her colour. In fact, she was one of the crowd now!

Story 2

Sammy the Tiny Elephant

"Hello, I'm Sammy. Yes, I'm down here." James looked round but couldn't see anyone. "I'm down by your feet. Ouch, you just kicked me!" cried Sammy. At that, James looked down and saw by his feet, the smallest, greyest elephant that he had ever seen, wearing a pair of tiny, red trousers. It was a perfect miniature of the big elephants he had seen at the zoo.

"Oh, I'm so sorry. I didn't meant to do that. I just didn't see you," said James. "Are you alright? Did I hurt you?"

"No," said Sammy, "but I do wish people would look where they put their feet."

"Why are you so small?" asked James, looking down again at Sammy.

"Oh, it's a long story. Do you want to hear it?" sighed Sammy.

"Yes please," replied James.

"Well, when I was a lot younger, I made the old witch, who lived in our village, very cross, so she put a curse on me. I will be small like this until I do a good deed for someone."

"Oh, you poor thing!" James cried, picking Sammy up and putting him on the wall beside him.

"H...e...l...p, I am too high, I will fall off!" wailed Sammy.

"No you won't. I will hold onto you," said James. "Are you alright now?"

"Yes, thank you. Oooh! It is so high up here. How do you manage to stay up here?" asked Sammy.

"Oh it's quite easy when you are big – ooops sorry," James told him. "Hopefully, you will be big again one day, then you will be able to sit here quite safely."

"I will never be big until I do a good deed for someone, but they never see me down here. I get kicked so much and people tread on me. I am black and blue all over some days. I am really afraid that I am going to be squashed and then I will never, ever become big," cried Sammy, as big tears started to run down his little trunk and drip off the end.

"Please don't cry Sammy. I will try and help you," replied James. "First we have to find something you can do as a good deed. Now, let me think......."

Sammy continued to sob big, silver tears. "What can I do? I am too small to lift anything. There is nothing I can do." His tears started to wet his little red trousers.

James quickly said, "We WILL find something, I promise. Come home with me and we will sort something out."

James lifted Sammy down off the wall and off they went. What a funny sight they were; a little boy and a tiny elephant in short, red trousers.

Suddenly, they heard a loud commotion and saw a lot of people running past. "What's happening? What's happening?" shouted James.

"There's a fire in Mr. Wilson's chicken house, the firemen can't get there as they are already out on another emergency!" yelled someone.

"What did he say?" asked Sammy.

"Apparently Mr. Wilson's chicken house is on fire....." began James, but got no further. On turning round, he couldn't see Sammy. Where on earth had he gone? James tried calling to him, "Sammy, Sammy, where are you?" All at once he heard a sort of loud trumpeting noise which seemed to be coming from the direction of the fire in Mr. Wilson's garden. As he ran towards the garden, an amazing sight met his eyes. In the garden stood a very LARGE, grey elephant (in short, red trousers), squirting water from the fishpond onto the burning chicken house! The flames were almost out. Sammy had saved the chicken house and the chickens! James starting dancing and yelling, "Good old Sammy! You are big again, you are BIG again!"

"Yes, and the witch's curse has been broken because I have just done a good deed," whispered Sammy. "Oh it is so great to be able to see over the top of things and no-one will step on me anymore."

"Um – yes that is great," groaned James, "but would YOU mind moving, because you are standing on my foot!"

Sammy laughed, "Oh dear, it will take me a bit of time getting used to being big again. Sorry!" Suddenly, people were coming over to thank Sammy for putting out the fire. He was very quickly getting used to being a 'Very Special Person'. "James, can I still come home with you, like you said please?"

James opened his eyes very wide, staring at the now, very BIG elephant..... "Oh crikey, yes I suppose so, but only for a little while and you will have to be very quiet because of our new baby." (James crossed his fingers behind his back.)

"I will be as quiet as a church mouse, I promise," answered Sammy.

James said, "Race you home!"

Mind you, he was wondering just how quiet a very large, grey elephant *could* be and what would his parents say.....? Off ran one little boy, closely followed by a LARGE grey elephant, in short red trousers. The ground shaking as he thundered along after James.

Everyone stood still, clapping and cheering. "Good old Sammy! Well done, you saved the chickens."

I do believe Sammy even did a little jump for joy, as he ran, because the ground shook even more!

Story 3

How Wilfred's Web Saved the Town

"Dum de dum, dum de dum," hummed a voice by the wall. "Wheee......!" On the word 'wheee', a big, black, hairy spider slid down a silken thread and landed with a bump. "Ouch, that hurt!" He looked very fierce, but really he was sort of big and fluffy and very friendly. His name was Wilfred. He was always ready to help anyone who needed it. Why, only the other day he had been able to mend the hole in the Mayor's white stockings!

"Dum de dum, dum de dum," sang Wilfred. "What shall I do today? I know, I will go for a walk as it is such a lovely day." With that, he popped into his hole in the wall and came out wearing his Very Best Hat. Now this was a fantastic hat; every colour of the rainbow with a big black bobble on the top. "Off I go to find some sun. Dum de dum, dum de dum."

He walked along the path by the river and stopped every so often to admire his Very Best Hat, reflected in the water. "Hello Mr. Blackbird, it is a beautiful day. Do you want to come for a walk with me?" asked Wilfred.

"Sorry, I would love to, but am helping the good lady spring-clean the nest," replied Mr. Blackbird.

"Never mind, maybe some other time. Cheerio," retorted Wilfred.

Off he strolled again, following the path up to the top of the hill and the big dam. As he got near the top, his eight legs started to feel tired, one after another. He decided to take the shortcut across the pipe that stretched across the top of the dam. "Yes that will save me quite a bit of time," thought Wilfred. He climbed very carefully towards the pipe so that he did not lose his Very Best Hat. Suddenly he found himself knee deep in water!

"Oh gosh!" cried Wilfred, "whatever has happened? It has not rained for days, but somehow I am all wet!" He looked down to where he was standing and saw a tiny fountain of water squirting out of the pipe, gradually getting bigger and bigger. "Wow, what shall I do? If this gets bigger, it will go 'pop' and then everyone will be washed away. The big people in the town down in the valley will be drowned. Oh dear, oh dear," wailed Wilfred. He then had a brilliant, nay, fantastic idea. He knew *exactly* what he had to do.

Very carefully he took off his Very Best Hat, (the one in rainbow colours with the black bobble on top) and laid it very carefully on a rock, out of reach of the water. Then he set to work to spin the best web he had ever spun in his life. He spun it back and forth, across the flow of the water, going over and over it to make it extra thick. He anchored it in so many places that it made it very difficult to climb over. The web grew bigger and bigger, thicker and thicker as he worked, and the water flow grew less and less until it stopped completely. "Whew, what a job!" said Wilfred, mopping his brow with one of his eight legs.

He peered at the leak. Yes, it appeared to be holding. "Oh good. I do hope it will hold until the big people can come up to mend it properly." Wilfred stood up and straightened his black legs, one by one by one by one by one by one by one by one. Mind you, he did have to wake three of them up because they had gone to sleep! He then picked up his Very

Best Hat and put it on his head. He adjusted it, after using a puddle as a mirror. Now what? He had to get help somehow. "I wonder if Mr. Blackbird would take a message down to the big people? Yes, I will go and ask him. He will probably be fed up with helping to do the spring-cleaning anyway."

Off Wilfred went, using one of his silken threads as a rope to swing down – he thought this would be quicker than walking, even on his eight legs. Down, down he went, holding onto his Very Best Hat, until he was level with Mr. Blackbird's nest. "Coo-ee, Mr. Blackbird, can you help me please? I have just stopped a leak in the pipe above the dam, but the big people in the town should know about it so they can mend it properly. Can you fly down to them with a message?"

"Why yes, of course I can," replied Mr. Blackbird. "I will write a note and put it through Professor Ambrose's window."

He disappeared indoors, found a piece of paper on which they wrote a note explaining about the leak. After folding it carefully, Mr. Blackbird picked it up in his beak and flew down towards the town in the valley.

He turned right at the bakery, left at the fish and chip shop, alighting on Professor Ambrose's windowsill. The window was slightly open, so he pushed the note inside, gave a quick tap on the glass and flew back up to where Wilfred was waiting. "Message safely delivered. Sorry I took so long," gasped Mr. Blackbird.

"Yes, I guessed you had delivered it because the big people are coming up the hill towards the dam already!" yelled Wilfred, pointing towards the line of big people, hurrying up the hill.

He threw his Very Best Hat into the air, caught it and put it back on his head. "I am going to watch them. Are you coming?" asked Wilfred.

"Yes, I don't mind if I do," replied Mr. Blackbird, fluffing out his feathers. Between them they had saved the dam, the big people and the whole village.

Story 4

The Day Mark's Shadow
Went Missing

There was once a little boy called Mark. He lived in the Big House, with his mother and father. The only trouble was he had no brothers or sisters to play with, so he was very lonely. He used to play with Topps, the gardener, until he became ill and had to go and live with his sister in Broadstairs. Miriam, the maid, was always far too busy (or so she said). The only other person he could talk to was Mrs. Moulqueen, the cook. He did not do that very often because she would 'box his ears' with her floury hands and shoo him out of her kitchen, if she was cross.

Poor Mark! He wandered round the Big House, sliding on the highly-polished floor in the Long Gallery, much to the annoyance of Miriam. (Well, what else was there for a boy to do......?) Anyway, they were only very tiny scratches on the floor, weren't they?

One day he was feeling very miserable and fed up. He had played all his games, been down to see Mrs. Moulqueen and got a floury clout for his cheek and had also been sent away by Miriam, who was cleaning the best silver, as she did not want his help. Mark decided to stop off in the Long Gallery. The sun was shining through the windows, making patterns and shadows on the floor. He looked at them and jumped onto one of the shadows on the floor – then a strange thing happened as he moved back into the sunlight. He saw that as he jumped, his body did not make a shadow anymore! Jumping back and forth into the sunlight, there still was no shadow! "Oh crikey, I have lost my shadow!" shouted Mark, suddenly feeling a bit frightened.

"No you haven't. It has gone to Misty Mountain," said a quiet voice. "If you stand quite still and shut your eyes, I will take you there and we will get it back."

Mind you, Mark already had his eyes tightly shut in terror. "Who are you? Where are you?" whispered Mark.

"Who? Me? You can open your eyes now Mark. My name is Porter because I am the porter that is sent out whenever anything is needed. Now, shall we go and find your shadow?"

At this, Mark suddenly remembered his parents, "What will my parents say when they can't find me?"

"Don't worry, they won't even realise you have gone because time goes faster in Misty Mountain than time here. You will be back before they blink. Ready?" Mark started to fidget. "You'll be perfectly safe. Just stand still please." Mark nodded, and there was a feeling of falling, which made Mark feel sick, but he kept his eyes screwed up tightly. He did not peep, even though he was now feeling very curious. "Ok, we are here," said Porter. "You can open your eyes now."

Mark slowly opened his eyes and stared. Everywhere was extremely bright. The trees were blue; the sky was green and the flowers – well, Mark had never seen anything like these strange flowers in so many weird colours. "Come please," said Porter, "we have a short walk to do." Looking at Porter carefully for the first time, Mark saw he was short, a bit tubby, but dressed in the weirdest coloured clothing. "Pray what are you staring at Mark?" said Porter, getting a bit agitated.

"You look so funny!" replied Mark, hoping he wouldn't offend the man.

"Oh boodledrops! You look funny to me as well!" retorted Porter.

In an instant Mark and Porter were surrounded by eerie mists which, when they cleared, showed they were at Misty Mountain. "Is my shadow in there?" queried Mark.

"Yes, the King collects them and changes them when he has finished with them," answered Porter. "This way. Let's go." Mark followed Porter down a long tunnel, which led to a very large cave which glittered with gold and precious jewels. The King sat on a gold throne at the far end of the cave.

"Who are you?" boomed the King in a deep, loud voice.

Porter bowed low. "If it please your Majesty, we have come to get Mark's shadow back."

"Oh I see, which one is yours, boy?" asked the King, turning to Mark.

Mark bowed low, "That is my shadow Sire," he answered, pointing to a shadow playing on the floor.

"How do I know it belongs to you boy?" the King asked.

Porter interrupted here. "Excuse me Sire, you will find that it will fit him perfectly."

The king nodded, "Alright, you may try it. You..... yes you, boy shadow! Come here please." The shadow came over and stood by the King. At a signal from Porter, Mark stepped over to the shadow in exactly the same position. "Bravo, they *do* belong to each other!" cried the King, clapping his hands together. "Well my boy, you may take your shadow and return home. I shall have to find another one now."

Bowing to the King again Mark said, "Maybe I can help you, Sire." He whispered to Porter, who clapped his hands and a beautiful lamp appeared. "Your Majesty, if you put something or someone between the lamp and the wall, you will have endless shadows." Mark showed the King what he meant.

"Oh how wonderful! Thank you *so* very much!" declared the King. "You are dismissed!" Porter and Mark bowed low, leaving the beautiful cave.

Porter said, "Mark, shut your eyes like you did before and you will be home instantly." Mark suddenly had the same feeling he had earlier. On opening his eyes, he found himself still in the Long Gallery, in the Big House. The sun was still shining and making shadows on the floor. When Mark saw this, he thought he would see if his shadow had come back. He stepped into the sunlight, and saw, to his relief – yes, his shadow was there! "It's back!" he yelled and danced for joy on the long, wooden floor. His shadow copying his every move!

"Whatever is the matter?" called his mother. "You have been very quiet and good up till now. What have you been doing?"

"You won't believe me mother, but I have been to get my shadow back!" said Mark happily.

"Nonsense!" said his mother. "You have been here all the time. Miriam saw you sliding on the floor. Anyway, come down and have your tea now."

Mark then knew that time *had* stood still here, but he was sure he had been away for hours and hours. "Thank you Porter," he whispered. He was thinking of his fantastic adventure and was *very* glad he had got his shadow back again.

Story 5

Duckling Love

The river was flowing fast and furious past the bottom of Paul's garden. He lived there with his mother and father and two sisters, Sally and Penelope, (Pen for short). It was a beautiful house with gardens sloping down to the water's edge. The children had a small boat which they played in during the summer. They also had a lolloping great dog that looked like a walking hearthrug. His name was Roamer because he had a bad habit of always wandering off! In addition to Roamer, the children had two white rabbits called Phil and Felicity, plus a big, white duck called Loveaduck, whose nickname was 'Love'. He had the run of the garden and, with the river to swim in, he was a very lucky duck!

Love used to come up to the back door for his meal each day, tapping on the door with his beak until Paul, Sally or Pen came out to him. He had his food in his own little dish, which he was very proud of. His favourite food was bread and milk, not too hot, not too sweet. Mind you, if he did not clear it all up, he would be helped out by Roamer – well, he was a rather greedy dog!

One day after school had finished, the children went out into the garden. Sally and Paul went over to let the rabbits out for a run. As usual Roamer was *all* over the place! How he missed treading on the rabbits one never knew.

"Where is Love?" asked Pen, looking under the fir tree where Lovaduck usually sat. "I can't find him."

"Perhaps he is out on the water?" volunteered Paul.

"Loveaduck, Loveaduck, where are you?" called Pen. Sally suggested that they took the boat out onto the river to see if they could find him.

"What a good idea, let's go!" said Paul.

The three children went down to the mooring, put on their lifejackets and got into the boat. Paul took the oars (he being the 'man' and also the eldest). "No Roamer, you can't come this time! Stay and look after the rabbits!" said Sally, struggling to push a reluctant 'hearthrug' back onto the bank.

"Right, which way do you think we should go?" asked Sally, pushing the boat away from the side of the bank.

Pen said, "Let's try 'Showboat Reaches' first. He must be somewhere." Slowly, they moved out into mid-stream with Paul rowing strongly against the current. As they got to 'Showboat Reaches', all the children began calling loudly.

"Loveaduck, come here, where are you?"

"Lovey, Lovey, where are you boy?"

Old Tom called from his boat where he was sitting, watching the world go by. "What's the matter?"

"Loveaduck has gone missing, and we are trying to find him. I don't suppose you have seen him?" asked Pen.

Tom scratched his head, "No m'dear, but I'll look out for 'e and let 'e know if I see him."

"Thank you Tom," the girls said in unison as Paul rowed off again. Their task had been a waste of time. They had looked into every mooring, and up every little creek, but no sign of Loveaduck.

"Shall we go the other way now?" said Paul, skilfully turning the boat around.

Choking back her tears Pen said, "Well we've *got* to try! Where can that silly duck have gone? He even missed out on his favourite bread and milk."

"Don't cry Pen, he will turn up I'm sure," replied Sally, putting her arm round her sister's shoulder. Paul rowed back along the river, past the bottom of their garden. Again and again they called Love's name, but there was no fluttering of wings or his favourite 'quack'.

"We had better go back now," Paul said quietly. "We can try again tomorrow."

"I do hope he will be alright," whispered Pen, wiping her eyes on her sleeve. Silently, they rowed back to their own landing stage and tied up the boat. Roamer came hurtling down the garden path to meet them, jumping up to greet them. "Get down Roamer, we haven't found him yet!" said Pen, crossly pushing him away.

"He will turn up, he has *got* to!" Sally said, with her fingers crossed tightly behind her back. "Come on, let's go and have some tea." They all trooped indoors, but did not have much appetite for food. "Whatever is the matter with you three?" asked their mother.

Penny began to cry, "Loveaduck has gone missing."

Her mother put her arms round her saying, "Don't cry Pen. Love often wanders, but he always comes back."

"We have been up and down the river, but couldn't find him," said Paul, playing with his bread and butter.

"Well, we can all try again tomorrow if he has not come back tonight," replied their mother.

Sally still had her fingers crossed under the table, "Yes he will come back soon," she said.

All evening the three children kept watch for Loveaduck and that night, three very quiet, sad children went to bed.

Next morning dawned bright and sunny and was also a Saturday, so no school. The children dressed quickly and ate their breakfasts as fast as they could. Even poor Roamer missed out on his usual titbits! The children ran out into the garden, down to the river's edge, but there was still no sign of Loveaduck. "He has *got* to be ok," said Paul bravely.

"Listen!" shouted Pen suddenly. "I'm sure I can hear something. Yes, it's Loveaduck – look!" and she pointed along the river. They all looked. A familiar 'quack-quack' was heard coming towards them. "He's back!" shouted Pen again, her eyes shining, "and look, he's got someone else with him!"

They stared and saw Loveaduck proudly waddling onto the path and behind him was another duck, but behind *her* were *seven* tiny, fluffy yellow ducklings, all running and flapping trying to keep up with the bigger ducks. "Hey, Loveaduck has got himself a lady duck and some babies!" yelled Paul.

"Mum, mum come and look," called Sally, "Loveaduck has got a wife and family!" She bent down to stroke Loveaduck, "Aren't you clever?"

Their mother came out, wiping her hands on her apron. "Oh Loveaduck, you have come home. No wonder you went away!" She also knelt down to coax the family. The babies were like little bundles of yellow cotton-wool and Loveaduck strutted about, every inch the proud parent!

Sally, cuddling one of the chirping babies in her hands, looked at her mother, "Mummy, can we keep them please, pretty please? We will all look after them, please mummy?"

Their mother looked thoughtful for a moment, "Well, I suppose we don't have any choice as they belong to Loveaduck. You will have to make up some sort of nest for them in the old boathouse where Loveaduck usually sleeps. Off you go then."

"Thank you mummy," said three children in unison. They ran off, calling Loveaduck to follow, who waddled after them, then he quacked to his little family to follow him!

What a lovely sight they made – three very happy children, a big white duck accompanied by his lady wife, and seven yellow, fluffy ducklings, running and flapping their tiny wings. They would be very comfortable in their new home…. A very puzzled Roamer stood watching them go down the path – what were those strange, yellow things he thought?

Story 6

Little Ossie's Visit to Hospital

"Mummy, it hurts so much!" cried Ossie, but he was trying desperately to blink back the tears.

"Yes darling, I know it does, but the ambulance will be here very soon, then the nurses and doctors will make it better. They are very kind," said Mrs Owl, putting her wing round her son's shoulders.

"What will they do? Will it hurt ever so, ever so much?" sniffed Ossie, wiping his beak on his feathers.

"The doctor who came to see you a little while ago said you had broken your leg, so I expect they will put it in plaster," replied Mrs Owl.

At this, tears began to run down Ossie's little feathered cheeks and he said, "I am so scared."

"There, there darling," whispered his mother, holding him gently to her. "I expect it will hurt a little bit, but they can give you something to help take away the pain. Listen, I think I can hear the ambulance."

All at once there was a knock at the door and there stood two blackbirds in uniform, carrying a stretcher. "Right 'o son, , we will put you onto this stretcher and carry you out to the ambulance. We will try not to hurt you too much." Ossie felt himself being gently and carefully lifted onto the stretcher and a big, warm blanket being wrapped round him. Ossie looked across to his mother and saw she was putting on her coat. Together they went out to the ambulance.

It was big and white, with a blue light on the top and filled with all sorts of strange things. Ossie, forgetting his broken leg for a moment said, "Will you have the blue light going round?"

The ambulance man turned to Ossie and smiled saying, "It depends on time and how much traffic there is. Ok Alf, you drive and I will look after our young patient." His mother sat on the opposite seat watching everything, anxiously.

The ambulance moved off quickly and Ossie found that he could still see out of the black windows. It went down the High Street and turned left into Watkins Street. After a little while they pulled up outside the hospital at a door marked 'Accident & Emergency'. Ossie was secretly sad that they did not use the blue light – oh well, never mind! The doors opened and his stretcher was wheeled into the hospital.

He was lifted gently onto a trolley. He heard his mother telling the lady at the desk who he was and what he had done. She gave them his name and where he lived. A nurse came over to him and started to push his trolley down the corridor. "Mummy, I want my mummy!" Ossie cried out. His mother hurried across to Ossie as he was wheeled into a special room called a cubicle. A very large owl was in there, wearing a white coat.

"Now young man, what have you been doing with yourself? I am Dr. Featherstorm at your service. Mmm, dear me," he said shaking his head. "Mmm, this looks like a small fracture. Have to get a picture of it before we do anything else. Porter!"

"Yes sir?"

"I have put a light support on this young man's leg, so can you please take him down to x-ray. Here are his notes.

I will be in here when you bring him back. See you shortly son," said the doctor.

"Right away sir," said the porter.

Ossie's trolley was then being wheeled along another white corridor, with his mother running behind, trying to keep up. They stopped outside a door marked 'X-Ray Department' in big red letters. The porter smiled at Ossie saying, "Here we are mate. The nurses will take extra special photographs of your poor leg and then I will take you back to the doctor."

A tiny nurse appeared and picked up his notes. "Oh yes, you are the young man with the broken leg. Well, first of all I am going to put you underneath a special camera. Then I will put a film in to take those special pictures. This will mean the doctor will be able to see where the break is, so he can mend it." She patted Ossie's wing gently. "You stay here Mrs. Owl, we'll not be very long."

Mrs Owl nodded and gave her son a quick kiss, "See you in a minute love." Ossie was pushed into the room full of large, noisy machines. He started to cry.

The tiny nurse put her wing round Ossie saying, "Please don't cry. This is the special camera. Watch what I do and then I will show you the pictures it has taken." Ossie watched carefully. The nurse set up all the pieces of machinery and put a special flat film under his leg. "Now lay *very* still. Ready?" He heard a whirring noise and then it was all over and the nurse came out from behind her special screen. "You can stay with your mummy in the other room while the pictures are being developed." She opened the big doors and pushed his trolley out into the other room, where his mother was waiting. Before you could shake your tail feathers, she was back with the special pictures!

"Is that the inside of my leg?" asked Ossie.

"Yes," the nurse replied, "and this is the break in your leg."

"It looks funny doesn't it mummy?" His mother nodded. The nurse then called the porter over, gave him the x-rays, asking him to take the patient back to Dr. Featherstorm.

Off they went again, down the white corridors, back to where they first came in.

"Hello young man, back again? Have you got your special pictures? Oh good." Dr. Featherstorm held them up to a special light. "Yes, mmm there is a small break. A fracture young man means a crack in your leg and we will have to put it in plaster for about six weeks." He looked at Ossie and smiled, "This plaster will support your leg until it heals." The doctor turned to the nurse saying, "Will you take Master Owl down to the plaster room and fit him with his cast?" and to Ossie he said, "You will soon be playing out again young man."

Mrs Owl stood up as the trolley was pushed down to the plaster room. This was different. It reminded Ossie of his art room at school – Plaster of Paris, bowls for mixing stuff in and so on.

"Oh what have we got here son? Oh, a broken leg!" said another doctor. He also looked at the x-rays. "That was a silly thing to do wasn't it?" Ossie nodded.

"Right, first of all we will straighten your leg, then we will put a special material on it before wrapping wet bandages round it. These will set hard and that is your plaster cast." Ossie was lifted onto a plastic sheet and he felt the doctor gently straightening his leg. He felt the strange material being put onto his leg, then another nurse started winding the wet bandages very gently round it. "Ugh, they're horrible and wet!" said Ossie, wrinkling his beak.

"Yes they will be for a few minutes, but soon they will be dry and hard," answered a nurse. "There, how does that feel young man?"

Ossie poked the plaster cast very cautiously – crikey, it had gone hard like rock! "Mummy, come and feel this," he said. His mother came over and tapped it gingerly.

When the plastering was finished, the doctor came into the room. "Good, excellent! Now Ossie, you are going to have to use some crutches to get around for a while." Ossie then saw the doctor had some things that looked like sticks in his hands. "Would you like to try using them?" He helped Ossie down from the bed and helped him put the crutches under his wings. Poor Ossie looked very worried, but managed to take a few wobbly steps. The plaster felt very heavy and awkward, but he turned to smile at his mother, saying, "Look, I can walk alright."

His mother said he was doing very well, but secretly hoped he would not get tangled up with them. She thanked the doctors and nurses, who said they would see him in six weeks to remove the cast. By the time Ossie and his mother got to the front door, he had managed to walk very well. "Race you mummy!" His mother laughed as she followed him – what a son, she thought............!

Story 7

Harriet and Toby's Moving Day

Harriet opened her eyes and blinked in the bright sunshine. She stretched, then looked across at her husband who was still snoring, blissfully unaware that today was *The Day*. Yes, today they really were moving down to the coast. She smiled to herself, then sprang into action. In her haste, poor Harriet got her slippers on the wrong feet; even her dressing gown was inside out! She poked her husband in the ribs saying, "Come on Bob, today is the day. It's lovely and sunny, and there's a lot to do!" A grunt from under the bedclothes was the only reply she got.

"Come on lazybones. If you don't shift, I will send the children in to get you up!" He heard her in the bathroom, singing, before going downstairs. Well, that threat did the trick! Bob knew from past experience that to be woken up by the children was sheer agony because they always insisted on tickling him, everywhere! He emerged from his pile of covers to find himself alone in the bedroom. He could hear Harriet busy downstairs, the children were making enough noise in their rooms to wake the dead!

"That's *my* shoe!" was heard from Alice.

"Come and get it then!" was David's taunting reply. Bob then heard a free-for-all start: crash, bang, wallop.

"Will you lot *please* shut up?" yelled Harriet. "You'll bring the ceiling down!"

Bob emerged from the bedroom, but when he opened the bathroom door, he found out why Toby their youngest child, had been so very quiet – everywhere was covered in toothpaste! He had squirted it on the mirror, over the bath and basin and even into the keyhole! What *would* Harriet say? Bob found the bath cloth and set about cleaning up the sticky mess. When he had finished, it did not look too bad, well maybe a bit smudgy, but definitely cleaner. Now to deal with the culprit.........!

He went downstairs and found his family eating breakfast. "When you have finished Toby, I want a word with you," Bob said. Toby looked up in surprise; what did his father want? When they had all finished, Harriet and Alice cleared away the dishes, washed and dried them, then packed them into the boxes. "Now Toby," said Bob, "why did you mess up the bathroom?"

Toby looked down at his shoes, then muttered, "I don't know.....," then slowly, "I don't *want* to move dad!"

Bob put his hand on Toby's arm, "Yes I know that son, but we have to. Just imagine being able to go to the beach whenever you like. There are times in life when one has to do things one does not like and this is one such time. Now go and finish the bits in your room because the removal men will be here soon."

Toby looked at his father, then stomped off back to his room. "I will run away! Yes, that's what I will do. I will go far away so they will never find me!" muttered Toby under his breath. Quickly he began to pack what he needed: first on his list was his favourite teddy, then his favourite marble. This was followed by a half-eaten packet of sweets, his best jumper, then last of all he emptied the money out of his moneybox. He wrapped everything up and placed them inside his school satchel, put on his coat and shoes and waited. He heard a lorry stop outside. When he looked out, it was the removal van and both his parents were outside with Alice and David. Now was his chance!!

He crept downstairs, out through the back door, pausing only to help himself to a packet of biscuits. Quietly, he opened the back gate and ran as fast as he could, until he had to stop and get his breath. Where was he going to stay he thought? The money he had added up to £4.49p. How about going to London? No, that would cost too much. Then he had a 'Good Idea', (Toby often had 'Good Ideas')! He would go to Aunt Jane's. She was his favourite auntie and lived at the big farm. The bus from the station passed it, so Toby set off to the village. The bus was already waiting at the station, so he got on and bought his ticket. The seats were fairly comfortable and he settled back to enjoy the journey.

As the bus got nearer to Aunt Jane's stop, he picked up his satchel. When the bus stopped Toby got off. Mmmm, this was the life; sunny and warm and the promise of a good time with Aunt Jane. Toby set off making his way up the track to the farm. He knocked on the door which was opened by his aunt. "Why Toby, what a surprise! What are you doing here?" Toby could smell that warm, delicious aroma of newly-baked bread which his aunt had been baking.

"I have run away!" stated Toby, "and I am never going back, not ever, ever again! So there!"

"Oh I see…..," remarked Aunt Jane, dusting flour from her hands. "Oh!" she said again, "well you had better come in, and we will have a little chat about this." Toby went into the kitchen and the smell of the newly-baked bread was making his mouth water. "Ooh that smells great!"

Aunt Jane took a still-warm loaf of bread, cut off a thick, crusty slice, buttered it and gave it to Toby. "Thank you very much," he said, taking a bite as the melting butter ran down his chin.

"Now young man, what am I going to do with you? Will you tell me why you have apparently run away?"

Toby mumbled, his mouth full of warm bread, "I don't want to move. I will miss all my friends."

Aunt Jane looked at him and said, "We have to tell daddy and mummy because they will be worrying about you. I will telephone them and see what we can work out, ok?" Toby nodded, tucking into another slice of the still-warm bread.

Jane went out into the hall and Toby heard her dialling a number. "Harriet, is that you? Yes, how are you?"

Toby quietly closed the kitchen door, keeping his fingers crossed. He shut his eyes tight, "Dear God, please let me stay with Aunt Jane and I promise I will go to the new house, and..... I will keep my bedroom tidy! Amen," he added as an after thought.

At that moment his aunt came back into the kitchen. "Have you finished your bread Toby?" He nodded. She continued, "I have spoken to daddy and mummy, they are very glad you are safe. Mind you, they are very cross because you ran away."

He hung his head and started to cry, "I am very sorry Aunt Jane, but I don't want to move."

Aunt Jane then said, "We know that love, but it was naughty to run away. Everyone was worried in case something bad had happened to you. Promise me you will not do that again?" Toby nodded again, wiping his eyes on his sleeve. "Good boy. Now, daddy and mummy have said that you can stay here with me for a few days until they have unpacked everything and sorted out your new bedroom. They will telephone me when they are ready, then I can take you over to the new house." Aunt Jane smiled, "You *will* get to like the new house, the same way you liked your old house."

"Yes, I suppose I will," agreed Toby reluctantly. "Aunt Jane, do you know what?" Aunt Jane shook her head. "Well, I am ever-so glad I did not run right away, or I would not be able to help you look after the animals, or have any of your super, warm bread, or........" At that, Toby suddenly jumped down from the chair and gave Aunt Jane such a *big* hug.

Aunt Jane hugged him back and smiled quietly to herself – "boys will be boys........!!"

Story 8

The White Butterfly

"Oh white butterfly, white butterfly, why did you fly, my white butterfly?" Abigail May Louise, (or 'Abby' for short, as she liked to be called), was muttering quietly to herself, but tears were running silently down her face and dripping off the end of her nose. What was the matter? What had made Abby so sad? She sniffed and rubbed her eyes which were red from crying. Suddenly a little voice spoke softly to her, "Why are you so upset Abby?"

Abby looked around, wiping a big teardrop off her cheek. To her amazement, on an upturned box, by the garden shed, sat a ...... well (she was not sure), but it looked like a....... yes..... a fairy? She stared hard at the small figure; no, she really *was* looking at a fairy! "Well?" asked the quiet voice, "what is the matter?"

"You are a-a-a-fairy!" spluttered Abby.

"Yes I am. My name is Fairy Snowdrop, and I have been sent here to find out why you are so sad," said the fairy.

Abby sat very still, open-mouthed, her tears forgotten. "How did you know my name?"

"We know everything about everyone in Fairyland; well almost everything," replied Snowdrop. "The Fairy Queen saw you were sad and sent me to help you. Pray tell me what ails you?"

Abby thought carefully before saying to Snowdrop, "I had a friend, a special friend," and she bent forward, continuing in a whisper, "an *extra special* friend."

"Tell me about your friend," Snowdrop said.

"Well, he was a butterfly. I found him as a furry, wriggly caterpillar. He used to tickle my hand when I held him." Abby laughed as she remembered this. "Anyway, one day I found he had changed into a hard, brown thing, which I did not like very much."

"That is a chrysalis," said Snowdrop.

Abby continued, "He was like this for a long time. I could not play with him. Then....." Abby frowned thoughtfully, poking out her tongue and wriggling it about, "then I came down one morning and he had changed again. He was a white butterfly, not a pretty one like daddy has in the garden. I did not think he was very nice so I shut him in a jam jar, but he died. I did not mean to kill him!" At this she started to cry again. "Daddy took him away."

Fairy Snowdrop again spoke very quietly to Abby, "But he did not die. He was brought to us, and even though he was nearly dead, we managed to save him and make him well again. You can see him for yourself if you wish hard enough."

Abby closed her eyes tightly and wished very hard, "*Please* let me see him again, please!"

As she made this wish, she felt something touch her hand very lightly. Opening her eyes she saw to her amazement, a beautiful white butterfly, HER white butterfly. "Oh you are beautiful, really beautiful," she said, "and I am very sorry for hurting you." The white butterfly flapped his wings gracefully and bowed his antennae.

"He says he was very lucky to be saved. He is now going to join his family in the fields and woods. He will fly back now and again so you can see him," Fairy Snowdrop explained. With that, the white butterfly stretched his wings and flew off from Abby's hand. He circled round her once then disappeared up into the clear, blue sky, off towards the fields and beyond. "Goodbye," whispered Abby to herself, "I will be waiting for you."

With this, Fairy Snowdrop spoke, "I shall also say goodbye. My work is done."

Abby looked down, "Thank you for saving him. I know now that even ordinary white things can be beautiful in a different way."

"You have learnt well Abby. Now close your eyes and sleep.....sleep......." Abby felt her eyes closing and soon she was fast asleep, curled up under the trees in the garden.

"Abby! Abby!" Abby suddenly woke up, hearing her mother calling.

"I have had *such* a strange dream mummy.............."

Story 9

The Timekeepers

Paul was asleep in his bedroom, snoring loudly as usual. He sounded like an express train roaring through a station: 'snort......snort......pheeew,.....snort, snort..... pheeew'.

"You *noisy* little boy!" shouted a voice. "Wake up! Wake up!" Paul woke with a start rubbing his eyes with the back of his hand. The voice said again, "You are a *very noisy* boy!"

"Pardon?" said Paul, who was now sitting up in bed, holding tightly onto his favourite teddy bear called Jackson.

"Oh, are you deaf as well as noisy?" asked the voice. Paul looked round his bedroom. He looked at the chair at the bottom of his bed. On it sat a little man, shimmering in a pale, blue light.

"Who are you?"

"I am called Eleven, like eleven o'clock," replied the little man.

"Gosh, what a weird name," replied Paul. "Where do you come from? What are you doing here?" He held onto Jackson a wee bit tighter!

The little blue man looked at Paul, saying, "What is wrong with my name? I think it's very nice! Anyway, why am I here? Well, I have been sent to try and stop you snoring." Eleven bowed. "You see, I live in the Land of Time. We work mainly on keeping all the clocks in the whole wide world going. I am called Eleven because that is my time for winding up the clocks." He bowed again. "The trouble is, I find I cannot get to sleep when I have finished winding because of your snoring. Even Eight and Nine complain! It's alright for Twelve because he is still awake!"

Paul shook his head, "I don't snore do I?"

"Yes you do," said Eleven, "listen!" At this, Paul heard what seemed to be the sound of a train rushing along. "*That* is you snoring!"

"Crikey, is that really me?" asked Paul.

Eleven nodded, "Yes it is. Now you can see why we have to try and make things a bit quieter for us." Eleven took his fingers out of his ears, "Come please." He beckoned, and Paul suddenly found himself floating out of his bed and out of his bedroom window, Jackson still held tightly in his arms.

In the twinkling of an eye they stopped in a lovely garden. "Where are we?" asked Paul, looking round. "Welcome to the Land of Time," answered Eleven, beckoning him towards a beautiful house. "This is our workshop where we live, work and sleep." As they entered, groups of little men and women, all dressed in the same shimmering blue as Eleven, gathered round. He cleared his throat. "You all know why Paul has been transported here?"

"Yes," chorused everyone.

"I've got a cure for his snoring!" shouted One. "Put him to bed later!"

"Hey, that's not fair," moaned Twelve. "That will mean I will not get *my* sleep, and you know I *must* have my beauty sleep!"

Six looked at Twelve, "It hasn't done much good for you so far!" ducking down as Twelve turned round quickly. Four appeared and nipped Paul's nose with his finger and thumb, saying, "Can't we put a peg on his nose?"

Paul rubbed his nose where Four had nipped it. "Ouch, that hurt!"

Eleven clapped his hands together, "Come, come men, now let us try and be sensible about this. Where is Ten?" They all looked round as an extremely old man came slowly into view, tottering towards the group of numbers, stopping in front of Paul.

He held out his hand, "Hello Paul, I am Ten. We appear to have a problem here and it includes you. My friends have some strange ideas on how to cure you of your snoring, but they will not work. My idea is simple, although I cannot guarantee that it will cure you completely. Take this little bottle," and he handed Paul a small, blue bottle. "Before you go to bed each night, rub some on your chest. It will help you breathe more easily, but it will only work for YOU!"

Holding onto Jackson, Paul took the small bottle and opened it carefully. He sniffed it cautiously; no it did not smell *too* bad, almost pleasant. "What happens when it runs out?"

Ten clapped his hands together, "It will *never* run out!"

"Ok, I will give it a try," said Paul. He put some in his palms and rubbed it onto his chest, "Mmm, that smells nice. Ten, Ten where are you...........?"

"Whatever is the matter love?" called his mother, coming into his bedroom. "You have been sleeping very well until just now. Gosh, what is that strange smell?" With that, she went across and closed his bedroom window.

Paul looked at his mother saying, "Ten gave me some stuff to rub onto my chest because my snoring was keeping all the people in the Land of Time awake. They keep all the clocks in the world going, you know. Ten said if I rub it on it would help me breathe and......."

His mother laughed, "Slow down Paul. You must have been dreaming. I think it's time for you to go back to sleep," as she bent over and tucked him in.

"Night, night mummy, I *wasn't* dreaming........" muttered Paul.

"Alright Paul, you were not dreaming. I believe you," said his mother, kissing him goodnight. "See you in the morning." Cuddling Jackson to him, Paul snuggled down again.

When his mother had closed the bedroom door, Paul opened his hand. In it lay a small, blue bottle.......no, he was sure that he had not been dreaming – after all, there was the small, blue bottle!

Story 10

The Bad-Tempered Crossword

In the compiling department of the local newspaper, Jason Conrad was sitting, thinking. He had a deadline to meet and the crossword puzzle he was working on was just not right! He looked out of the window and noticed that it was starting to get dark. Rain was beginning to fall. "Oh what an awful night it's going to be," he thought, idly tapping a cup of cold coffee, making ripples run across the surface. A piece of sticky doughnut fell off the desk onto the floor. "Oh bother!" yelled Jason, picking up the paper with the half-finished crossword on it. He threw it into the wastepaper basket. He felt so tired now. What would the Editor say tomorrow – no crossword meant no more work and no pay! Jason put his head down on his arms, on his desk, and closed his eyes. "Maybe I will feel better if I have a nap," he thought. Within minutes he was fast asleep.

He was suddenly aware of a rustling by his side. It seemed to be coming from his wastepaper bin.

"No, I must be dreaming."

But Jason could not resist it any longer as the noise grew louder. He looked down and in the bin was his unfinished crossword, but all the letters he had already written on it had vanished!

"Don't just sit there looking at us. Tip the bin out onto your desk!"

Jason was so amazed that he did just that. Out fell bits of torn-up paper, a pile of individual letters, a couple of empty biros, crisp packets, oh, and the piece of sticky doughnut. "That's better. Now we can see what we are doing." The voice apparently belonged to a letter 'A'. Jason stared. "We have decided to help you with the crossword problem you appear to have. We also know why you have not been able to complete it!"

"Good grief, talking letters! I must be going mad!" muttered Jason.

"No lad, you're not going mad. All day you have been pushing us about in the squares. Some of the words you made were just *so* silly, we just have to help you," said 'A'. Jason could only nod his head up and down like a cork bobbing on water.

'A' started speaking again, "Now, that last word you could not work out, number 17 across, it was POSTER. You see, letters 'D' and 'R' had an argument as both of them wanted to finish the word. So they decided to have a contest to see who was the best letter. In the end 'R' won, but 'D' kept hiding the square. This was why you could not finish your crossword."

"Ok, but what can I do? What are *you* going to do?" asked Jason. "I have to have this finished and on the Editor's desk first thing tomorrow morning, or I will not have a job."

"Leave it to us lad," 'A' replied. "You go home and don't worry. Everything will be fine. Go on, *go, shoo*!"

Jason stood up, put on his mac, turned off the lights saying as he went, "Good luck!"

As soon as the door closed, things began to happen; magic things.................. Letters flew this way and that, letters standing on letters to make big words. As 'Dot' was not needed, he kept checking the spellings in the dictionary. "No, it is 'I' before 'E' except after 'C', not the way you two are standing; 'Q', I know you usually have to go with 'U', but in the word 'uncle', you do not have to stand together." So, it went on all night until daylight started to creep through the windows. "Right lads, are we all finished?" called 'A', as he looked at all the black and white squares. They were all full of letters, making up sensible words. "That is a *good* night's work!" he said.

When Jason came into his office in the morning, everything seemed to be just as he had left it yesterday – the cold cup of coffee by his pencil and the wastepaper bin standing by the side of his desk. He looked into it. The screwed-up paper seemed to still be in there. A wave of panic went through him...... "They hadn't done it! What was he to do now?"

"Good morning JC!" boomed Mr Atherton, the Editor. "I've had a look at this crossword and I must say it's one of the *best* you have done! Can you get it down for printing immediately lad please?" He handed Jason the crossword, as he left the office.

Jason examined it closely – why, they HAD finished it and it looked bigger and better that ever before! He looked at number 17 across, and it said 'POSTER'. They had even sorted out that spelling!

He whistled as he took the crossword down for printing. What a strange night it had been.............!

Story II

Emergency at the Yard

The old coach station hummed with activity. Faded and peeling paintwork had been cleaned and re-painted a lovely blue colour. The windows had been polished until they sparkled like diamonds. Even the pathways had been scrubbed! The window boxes had been painted brilliant white and were filled with beautiful, coloured flowers. Red, white and blue flags hung everywhere. It looked a picture, ready for the 'Special Event', which was due at 10 o'clock tomorrow.

In the corner of the yard stood a very shiny, new bus, Number 1777. He was going to lead the 'Special Event'. This was to take the Lord Mayor and his guests to the opening of the New Town Hall and the Transport Museum.

Now, you would have thought that Number 1777 would have been very happy to have this very great honour; well, he wasn't! Steve, the driver, came over to Number 1777, saying, "You look very miserable. Come on, cheer up! The Mayor will be here tomorrow and you will be leading the procession."

Number 1777 coughed and spluttered, then spluttered and coughed again, "I do not feel very well, I *am* sorry."

He seemed to shiver. "I am too ill to lead the procession. You will have to get someone else to do it."

"Ok, so you don't feel well. What on earth do we do now?" asked Steve. "Who can we use to lead the procession if you cannot do it? There is no-one here who is as smart as you!"

"Me-e-e-e-me, I can, I can!" called a small voice. Steve turned and looked towards a little, country bus. These buses were originally called 'charabancs' and were used in large numbers to take people on holidays, about forty or fifty years ago. They had not been used since the newer, more up-to-date coaches had been brought into service.

The little, country bus was nicknamed 'Monty'. He was dusty, with cobwebs hanging across his dirty windows like lace curtains. Rust patches discoloured his paintwork, the headlights were hanging off; the door was leaning against the side! He looked a very sorry sight....... Steve laughed, "YOU can? Don't be daft! Just look at the state of you; you are nothing but a heap of junk!" and he thumped his big hands onto Monty's bonnet.

Monty sneezed, "Yes, I know I'm a bit of a mess now, but with a wash and polish, plus a fresh coat of paint, I will be honoured to take the Mayor and his special guests to the New Town Hall tomorrow. Please let me, please, please!"

Steve scratched his chin thoughtfully, "Alright, I tell you what we will do. It will not be dark for another three or four hours, so we will see. *If* we can get you looking smart and tidy by tomorrow morning, you can take the Mayor in the procession. Only *if* you are smart enough!"

Monty shuffled his wheels about and they creaked a bit because he had been standing around for a long time. "Thank you very much."

Steve set off to the workshop and came back with buckets of water, mops, tins of paint, oil, screwdrivers, polish, and all the other engineers. They started undoing nuts and bolts, squirting oil everywhere, into every nook and cranny they could find. Someone else was taking down the cobwebs, whilst others were underneath clearing the grass which had grown up level with Monty's doors. His tired and rusty wheels were taken off and replaced with new, shiny ones. He could also feel someone else running water over his dirty paintwork and scrubbing him with the mops. The tins of paint were then opened; he could smell it as they started to paint him. Time passed far too quickly and they still had *such* a lot of work to do if they were to get Monty ready for tomorrow.

Steve sighed, "Oh Monty, we will never manage to do it in time! We're all *so* tired! We *must* have a little sleep, but we'll be back very early tomorrow morning to try and get you ready."

"Ok," whispered Monty. "Goodnight Steve, thank you everyone." All the engineers nodded and left for home.

Suddenly the Yard was very quiet.....

A green glow seemed to hover around the spot where Monty stood in disarray, making the whole yard seem strangely magical. It moved upwards, then began to move over and around him, making Monty feel *very* strange. He felt very sleepy, so he closed his eyes, (well, they were actually his headlights) and...........

"Hey man, what's happened?"

"Crikey, it's flipping miracle!"

Monty woke with a jerk! What on earth was all the noise and shouting about? He had been having the best sleep for ages. "Monty, Monty, what has happened to you?" yelled Steve. "Just look at you!"

Monty looked and could not believe his eyes. He saw shiny, new paintwork and sparkling windows; his new seats smelled of real leather; his headlights really did shine like diamonds. "Wow, is it really me?"

Steve then said, "Now you *can* lead the Mayor's Parade Monty! You will do us proud!"

Monty hooted his horn, "Yes I will! *Toot, toot!*"

Steve and the other engineers still could not believe their eyes. Was this really old Monty who had been covered in cobwebs and all rusty yesterday? Steve took a duster out of his pocket and lovingly rubbed a speck of dust from one of the door-handles. "Well Monty, it looks as if you have passed, so are we ready to go?" He climbed up into the driver's seat, started up the engine, and moved off slowly. He drove Monty down into the main yard where all the flags were fluttering in the breeze. He stopped in front of the Mayor, who looked very grand in his top hat and tails, with his official gold chain. "So this is my official transport?" boomed the Mayor. "It looks fantastic! I have not been on one of these since I was a little boy. You have done it up beautifully." He walked right round Monty, looking at the fresh paintwork and sparkling windows. "Super!" he said again as he climbed aboard, followed by the Lady Mayoress and the other V.I.P. guests.

Steve moved off feeling very proud and important in his uniform. Monty felt very important as well. Who would have thought that strange and wonderful things could happen over-night?

But then Monty believed in magic – do you?

Story 12

The Magic Glasses

Eric was walking slowly along the lane, not far from the bottom of his garden. He idly kicked some stones and then booted an empty drinks can as well. 'Clank, p'dong, clank, clash, clash', it went as it rolled down the road. It made this odd sound because it was bent out of shape. Eric kicked it again, but this time he did not kick it quite right because his shoe flew off! It flew up into the air and over the hedge. "Ooops!" thought Eric.

He climbed through a hole in the hedge and started looking for his shoe. It had landed on a grassy bank. Eric bent down to pick it up, but had to sit down and tie up his laces. When he bent down he noticed a funny little pair of glasses lying partially hidden in the grass. He picked them up and looked at them. They were small and silver- coloured with round eyes. "I wonder who they belong to?" Eric thought, turning them over in his hands. He put them into his pocket because he was going to take them to the police station, as he had always been told to take anything valuable there. He would take them in on the way home!

Like all young boys, Eric still idly kicked stones along the lane and, before he realised it, he was back home. Suddenly, he remembered he had not called in to the police station with the glasses! His parents were sitting in the garden in the sun. "Hi," he called.

"Oh, hello son," said his father. "If you care to give your hands a wash, you can have some of this cake and a drink," pointing to a lovely fruit cake that was on a plate.

Eric replied, "Right ho, won't be a sec," and ran indoors. He went up to the bathroom and carefully washed his hands. He looked in the mirror – and suddenly remembered the glasses again! Taking them carefully from his pocket, he tried them on.....

All at once he could 'see' and 'hear' his parents sitting in the garden, and they were talking..... "Do you think we should tell him yet, darling?"

"Yes, when he comes down. I hope he'll not mind if it's a little sister because he's always wanted a little brother."

Eric was puzzled. He took off the glasses and looked at them. Strange, he thought, they looked quite ordinary. Maybe he had imagined it? So he put them on again. Instantly, he could see his mother and father laughing and holding hands. Gosh, what were these glasses doing? Taking them off yet again, he took them over to the sink, rinsed them, gently dried them on the towel, then put them back into his pocket. Opening the door, he ran downstairs and out into the garden.

His parents were drinking tea. "We have some good news for you," said his mother, smiling at her husband, "you are going to have a new baby brother or sister."

Eric was pleased, but did add that he 'hoped it would be a brother', stating this between mouthfuls of cake.

As his parents took the plates and cups back indoors, Eric took a quick look at the glasses and carefully put them on again. This time he could 'see' his mates down by the river, fishing. Suddenly he realised that he had *actually* been *thinking* about them, wondering what they were up to. Maybe the glasses had the power to make thoughts appear in reality? He tried thinking about his brother, who was away in the R.A.F., and found he could 'see' Michael in his room, cleaning his shoes and whistling tunelessly, (as usual). "These are brilliant!" thought Eric. Casually, he began to think about his gran, whom he loved very much. Almost immediately, he could 'see' her, making herself a cup of tea in her little kitchen. "Yes, these glasses were definitely magic – maybe they would be useful sometime?" and with that, he slid them back into his pocket.

All lovely, long, summer evenings eventually turn to night time and Eric soon found himself being advised that it was his bedtime, as he had school tomorrow.

'Ring, ring' went the alarm, standing on Eric's bedside cabinet. It was suddenly 7.30am and he woke with a start. He felt under the pillow. Yes, the glasses were still there, so he transferred them to his school bag.

He dived into the bathroom before running downstairs for his breakfast. "Don't forget gran is coming over tonight," said his mother, straightening his tie and trying to flatten the piece of hair that always insisted on standing up! "Off you go!" Eric kissed her goodbye, picked up his school bag and then caught up with his best mate Jason, (who preferred to be called Jay). He couldn't resist showing Jay the small glasses.

"Cor, put 'em on Eric. Let's see 'em on you; give us a laugh!"

"Ok!" replied Eric, doing just that.

As he did so, he found he was 'seeing' his grandmother, who seemed to be rushing about in her kitchen. Suddenly, she put her hand up to her chest, appeared to cry out, then fell to the floor! Eric grabbed Jay's arm and shouted, "Come on, my gran has been taken ill!" And with that the two boys dashed off.

Poor Jay was soon out of breath. "Hold on a sec!" he gasped. "How do you *know* she's not well?"

"It's these glasses!" panted Eric. "Whatever I think of when I am wearing them seems to become real." And they raced onwards.

They turned into gran's road, vaulted over the low, garden wall, which ran down the side of the house towards the kitchen. As they pushed open her back door, they both saw her lying there on the floor. Her face was white with pain and she was breathing in small gasps.

"Oh thank goodness someone is here! Please ring for the doctor, I feel so ill!" she whispered.

Eric knelt down beside his gran and held her hand. "Hello gran, it's me, Eric. Lie still, and we will get help." They first of all rang '999' for an ambulance. Jay went into the lounge to get a cushion to put under her head and the blanket from the settee. "You'll be alright gran, I know you will!" Eric said, still holding her hand tightly.

They heard the ambulance arrive and two paramedics came to the back door. "Alright my love, we will soon have you settled," they said, as they very gently did some medical treatment, lifted her onto the stretcher, then took her out to the ambulance. "Do you think you can contact your mum?" one of them asked. Eric and Jay both nodded.

"Did you really 'see' this happen?" asked Jay as they followed gran's neighbour indoors. She had come round immediately she saw the ambulance to see if she could help in any way.

"Yes, it was these glasses." Eric took them out of his pocket, but they were broken in two and the lenses had shattered! There was nothing to see now, no magic; they were just...... ordinary.

Jay thought aloud, "Maybe they were only meant to work so we could save your gran's life?"

"Mmm, maybe that was the magic......." replied Eric.

Story 13

Martin Millipede's Mishap

'Tap, tap, tap, tap, tap, tap, ouch! Tap, tap, tap, tap, tap, tap, ooh!'

Martin Millipede was walking very carefully indeed – tap, tap, tap, tap, tap, tap. "Oh dear..... It's no good," he said. He sat down with a thud, on a clump of grass. "Oooh, that's better." He crossed his leg, his leg, his leg, in fact all fifty of them, (actually he was not too sure just how many legs he *did* have!)

Suddenly, a rather posh voice spoke to him, "Ahem, excuse me, but you are sitting in my doorway and I cannot get indoors." Martin looked round and saw a little, black mole. The mole continued, "I say old chap, one has to get home to the little wife and kids you know. Oh by the way, are you having trouble?"

"I'll say I am. My seventh and eighth feet are *so* sore," replied Martin. "I just do not know how to put one foot, one foot, one foot, one foot, in front of the other. You see, I had all my shoes repaired yesterday, and for some reason, two of them are really giving me such pain. I cannot take much more of it, but, like yourself, I must get home to the missus, yet I don't know how. Oh, by the way, let me introduce myself, Martin Millipede at your service. Who do I have the pleasure of addressing?"

The small mole gave a little bow, "I am Sebastian Marmaduke Golightly, but my friends all call me 'Marmy'. May I take a look at the shoes which are causing you pain?"

Martin lifted up his foot, his foot, his foot, his foot. "No not that one, or that one, or that one; oh yes, these are the two causing me the pain," he said holding up two of his fifty little feet, which were all clad in small, black shoes. He bent over and removed them, "Ah bliss!"

Marmy took the little black shoes and sat down. He turned them over and over in his hands very carefully and felt inside them. "I have it!" he exclaimed. "I know the reason why your shoes are hurting you so much. The insides of the shoes do not seem to match up with the tops, and the stitching of the 'watcha-ma-call-it' is far too lumpy! Mmm, now what can I do?" He scratched his head thoughtfully, ouch! He'd forgotten he had a shoe in his hand! "Oh gosh, I am such a clever, clever Marmaduke, I have got *just* the thing! Spare winter coats!"

"Beg your pardon?" interrupted Martin.

Marmy stood up saying, "Have you got time to come down into the happy home? The little wife will make a nice pot of tea and she could even have some hot, buttered toast ready! Then, whilst you have some of that, I will solve your sore feet problem. What do you say?"

"Well, if you insist, and you think can sort them out, I would be honoured to share your table. Onwards Marmy!" Martin said, getting up and following his new friend down into his home. All you hear now was 'tap, tap, tap, tap, tap, tap, *hop*; tap, tap, tap, tap, tap, tap, *hop*....'

They went along what seemed to be miles and miles of tunnels, with Marmy stopping every so often to greet friends and introduce Martin at the same time. "Here we are, home, sweet home." They had arrived at a little, round door which Marmy pushed open. The smell of bread baking wafted out, mingling with the sounds of children, laughing. Suddenly, four children bounded out and ran up to Marmy, all trying to kiss him! "Steady on!" cried Marmy, disappearing under masses of arms and legs. "Look, I have brought a friend with me. Can I introduce Martin Millipede? Martin, these are my adorable children, Marion, Martha, Mary and Sebastian the younger."

The children stopped and looked at Martin. "I am very pleased to meet you all." The children all shook his proffered hand.

"Right ho, where's my favourite lady?" asked Marmy, ushering everyone inside so he could close the door.

"Hello my dearest," called a voice, as a sweet little lady mole came out of the kitchen, drying her hands on a towel and giving her husband a warm kiss. "I am Hetty, pleased to meet you."

"Hetty, this is my friend Martin Millipede. He has been having trouble with some of his shoes and I have had a really super idea how we can help him. I did say you might be able to rustle up a pot of tea and some hot, buttered toast whilst I sort them out."

"Of course, do come in," replied Hetty. "Children, can you please clear a chair for our guest?" They all went into the lovely, warm kitchen where Hetty and the children laid out a crisp white tablecloth, put some cups and plates on it, full of hot, homemade bread, scones, butter and scrumptious strawberry jam. This was followed by a large pot of tea.

Marmy called out, "I won't be a minute Martin. Please help yourself to food."

In a flash Marmy had vanished. Hetty and the children sat down at the table, offering Martin some tea and a choice from the loaded plates in front of him. They all chattered away, nineteen-to-the-dozen, enjoying the feast. Time flew by so quickly that Martin did not realise Marmy had returned with his shoes. Marmy held them up triumphantly, saying, "Here you are my friend! Please try them on, see how they feel."

Martin bent down and carefully put them on – yes, they felt absolutely comfortable, really, absolutely super-duper comfortable! "How have you managed to make them so comfortable?"

"Well, I have lined them with our old, fur coats. As you probably realise, our coats get very muddy and dirty down here in the tunnels, so we have lots of coats to change into. It is such a waste seeing them lying about not being used," smiled Marmy.

"Bravo! Well done!" chorused Hetty and the children. "You are so clever!"

"Yes, I really do not know how to thank you. They are so soft now," Martin said, wriggling his toes.

Marmy shrugged, "Oh it was nothing. Has anyone left me any tea?" He sat down at the table feeling very pleased with himself. They all ate and drank tea, told jokes and stories and had a lovely time.

At last Martin stood up, "I really *must* be going. Thank you for your wonderful hospitality, especially for repairing my shoes." He kissed them all goodbye and shook hands with Sebastian Senior and Junior. Marmy then escorted him back to the surface.

"Goodbye my friend and thank you once again." Martin set off towards his house and this time all you could hear was 'tap, tap, tap, tap, tap, tap, oh bliss; tap, tap, tap, tap, tap, tap, oh bliss'.

Just remember, if you see a millipede walking about with a silly smile on his face, it is all down to his seventh and eighth shoes being lined with soft, black velvet. And you can bet his name will be Martin!

Story 14

The Angel Who Polished the Stars

Sarah Elizabeth sat looking out of her bedroom window. How brightly the moon shone; it made her pink quilt-cover look almost silver. The stars were also starting to slowly peep out and they sparkled like diamonds, lying on a piece of black velvet. She sighed quietly to herself, "Oh how I wish I could hold a star in my hand and see it sparkle. It must be like holding a piece of heaven."

Sarah Elizabeth walked slowly back and got into bed. She snuggled down under her quilt, having first picked up her favourite toy rabbit called 'Whiskers'. She called him Whiskers because he had very long, soft, silky whiskers and a white fluffy tail. "Night, night, Whiskers," she murmured, turning over and popping her thumb into her mouth as she closed her eyes.

"Sarah Elizabeth! Sarah! Wake up, it's your turn at 'star duty'." Sarah Elizabeth rubbed her eyes and looked round. All she could see was a very bright light and hundreds of people hurrying about. She hugged Whiskers tightly. A beautiful

50

lady was standing by the side of Sarah Elizabeth. "Where am I?" asked Sarah, "this isn't my bedroom and *you* are not my mummy! I am scared!" She started to cry.

"Hello Sarah Elizabeth, I am Paola and I am an angel. Well, actually I am still earning my wings," she said turning round to show Sarah two tiny wings on her back. "Then, when I pass my exam I will get my proper wings."

Sarah Elizabeth asked Paola, "What are they like, these proper wings?" She was not quite so scared now. She noticed that the other people all appeared to have wings; large ones, small ones, white ones, silver ones and even gold ones.

Paola pointed to some large, white wings on a person walking past saying, "Mine will be like those."

"Oh, I see, but what am *I* doing here?" asked Sarah Elizabeth again.

"Well, you wished you could hold a star in your hands and we have decided to help you," replied Paola. "Come, we have much work to do." As she took Sarah Elizabeth's hand very gently, they both started to float down into a big, white room. Sarah Elizabeth suddenly panicked, "What about my mummy? She will be very worried when she finds I am not in my bed!"

"Please do not worry, Sarah Elizabeth. We have left your 'shadow image' in your bed, and besides, time is very different here," Paola replied. They floated down and down, stopping by a beautiful glass door. Very quietly the door slid open and Sarah Elizabeth saw a room which was even more beautiful. It sparkled like millions of diamonds; fantastic colours flickered round the walls.

"Wow, it is so-o-o beautiful!" gasped Sarah Elizabeth, "what is this room Paola?"

"This is the room where the stars are polished every night, before being put out into the night sky," replied Paola, guiding Sarah Elizabeth round the room. "Here we have the stars that are too small to go out into the night sky. They stay here for years and years until they are big enough. We call it our 'star nursery'." Sarah Elizabeth peeped in and saw thousands of stars twinkling away, very tiny stars.

"Next is where the 'dirty' stars come in to be cleaned. They arrive here each morning after being out in the sky all night, see?" Paola continued, handing Sarah Elizabeth a star. It was so grey and dull, "You would not be able to see that if it was put out again tonight."

Sarah Elizabeth looked again at the star in her hand, "Please may I clean this one?"

Paola nodded and took her across to some special boxes. "Put your star onto that dish and then put it in the box." Sarah Elizabeth did as she was told. "Right, now press that red button and the machine will start working." She did that as well, and the machine started working ..... 'sssh, plop, sssh, plop'. A green light then flashed at the far end of the machine.

"That means your star is clean and now just needs polishing," said another angel, standing there at the far end.

Sarah Elizabeth opened the door and took out the dish with her star on it. Yes, it did look a bit cleaner, but it did not sparkle like stars should. "What happens after this?" she asked.

"Now we will go down to the polishing department," was Paola's reply, leading her along another passageway into yet another room. Here, all Sarah Elizabeth could see were boxes and boxes of glitter. They reminded her of the glitter you get on Christmas cards. Angels, with different coloured wings, were busily polishing stars until they shone. These polished stars were so bright, they almost hurt Sarah Elizabeth's eyes to look at them! Paola picked up a star from a box, then picked up a handful of glitter and began rubbing it. As she rubbed it, the star seemed to glow, and the longer she rubbed it, the brighter it became. When she had finished, she laid it very carefully on a soft, black surface and turned to Sarah Elizabeth saying, "That is all you have to do with your star. You can rub it with gold or silver glitter or both if you wish, whichever you like to choose."

Sarah Elizabeth put her dish down and picked up her star, together with a handful of glitter, some gold and some silver, and started to rub. At first nothing appeared to be happening, but then, as if by magic, it started to shine. Oh, how beautiful her star was now – it shone like a diamond! She turned to Paola, "Do I put it in here now?"

Paola nodded saying, "This is now your very own special star." Sarah Elizabeth carefully laid her star onto the soft, black surface nearby.

Suddenly a tinkling bell sounded and all the angels quietly made their way to the benches, covered with sparkling stars. A window silently slid open and then thousands and thousands of stars seemed to float and glide effortlessly out into the night sky. Sarah Elizabeth watched in amazement at this and could see that HER special star was the brightest! Well, so SHE thought!

"This is for you dear Sarah Elizabeth," and as she turned round, Paola gave her a tiny, white box. Inside were the most delicate pair of wings she had ever seen and Paola seemed to be wearing some *large* wings now!

"Thank you so much, they are truly beautiful," whispered Sarah Elizabeth.

"Now we must go home," explained Paola. "When you look out into the night sky, you will be able to see your 'special' star tonight." She grasped Sarah Elizabeth's hand and they floated up and up into the air. (If only she could float to school like this she thought!) "How will I know my star amongst all the thousands of others out there?"

"You will because it will be the brightest one in the sky. Look for it when you are ready for bed tonight," said Paola, kissing Sarah Elizabeth goodbye and at that moment, everything changed…. She found herself back in her own bed, with Whiskers in her arms. Paola had vanished – was it a dream? There was only one way to find out the truth. She crept quietly to the window and looked out into the night sky. It was full of stars. Suddenly she saw a beautiful star – it was silver and gold and sparkled very, very brightly – yes, that was HER special star!

She closed the curtains and went over to her bed. Lying on the quilt cover was the box Paola had given her and on opening it..... well, can you guess what she saw inside.....? Yes, the pair of tiny wings were nestling and glittering there.

Well, it couldn't have been a dream, could it?

Sarah Elizabeth was not sure.

Maybe in the morning she would decide...........

Story 15

The Muddled Clock Numbers

"Oh for goodness sake, we *must* get this straight! NINE comes a long way after THREE. In fact, you are a whole thirty minutes after!" Ben Bigg, who was in charge of the clock-making department, poked NINE. "I have shown you the picture where your position is. Can't you remember?"

"Er well..... I have a bit of a cold today and I keep standing on my head," snuffled NINE. "In fact, a little while ago, I thought I was SIX when I could not get upright."

"Typical, trying to copy me because I am the greatest!" called SIX.

Number NINE sniffed, "No I wasn't, I just did not feel well."

"Can you use a hankie?" yelled EIGHT. "I *don't* want your germs!"

"Well, neither do I," piped up TEN, "but we have no choice. He is always between us and whenever he is ill, *we* seem to catch it. I wish he would change places with FOUR or something!"

At that FIVE turned round and said, "Hey come off it! Why should I get lumbered with him? You know I don't like him, he's not *my* friend. FOUR is my best friend."

Ben Bigg turned to FIVE, "Look, NINE cannot possibly be next to you because the time would not be right. Can you imagine what a muddle everyone would be in?"

"What do you mean?" asked NINE, sniffing again, pulling out a very large, white handkerchief with red spots on it.

"Oh look at that!" shouted EIGHT, pointing to NINE's hankie. "It looks like something that might be catching!"

NINE sneezed and with a fierce look on his face, said, "If you don't shut up, I'll clock you one!"

"Boys, boys!" chimed Ben Bigg. "It's a lovely handkerchief NINE. At least he uses one, not like *some* people I know!" At that, he let his gaze wander round the assembled numbers. A few of them shifted their feet around, looking down at the floor. "Now, as I was about to say a little while ago, if you do not go to your correct places on the clock dial, time will not make sense at all. For example, you could not have quarter *to* the hour with NINE over by FOUR, and you could not have twenty minutes *past* the hour with FOUR over in NINE's place; it just would not work. The clock face has been exactly the same for hundreds of years and we cannot change it now." The assembled numbers nodded their heads in agreement.

"Atishoo! Atishoo! Sorry!" mumbled NINE.

"Bless you my son," said TWELVE, who had also wandered in at the end of the earlier conversation. TWELVE had a calm look on his face because he was the eldest of the numbers. "I heard all the shouting, so I thought I had better come in and see why," he said.

Ben Bigg came over to TWELVE and explained the situation, "No-one wants NINE by the side of them because he has a cold, but he has to go between EIGHT and TEN, or time will be wrong."

"It's only a cold-in-de-dose," muttered NINE again.

A door opened and TWO, THREE and FOUR came in holding hands, laughing and singing. "I don't know why you are all so cheerful!" moaned NINE, "perhaps it's because *you* haven't got pneumonia like me!"

TWO, THREE and FOUR all spoke at once, (they always did everything in three's). "Pneumonia?" said TWO.

"Pneumonia?" said THREE.

"Pneumonia?" said FOUR.

NINE sneezed, "Yes, dat's right, pneumonia and influenza as well! No-one wants me to be by their side on the clock face because of this!"

TWELVE stepped over ELEVEN and SEVEN who were fast asleep in the corner. "I know what will cure your cold!" He looked at ELEVEN and SEVEN thinking, "Those two could sleep anywhere! The only time ELEVEN wakes up is when the chimes are due at eleven o'clock and as for SEVEN, well, he's always tired!" SEVEN slept every spare minute because he was the early riser when humans wanted to set their alarms at seven o'clock – poor SEVEN!

TWELVE came back with a large can of oil, "A squirt of this will cure you NINE! Open wide!" he said.

NINE opened his mouth and swallowed hard, "Mmmm that tastes nice. Gosh my cold does seem to be improving!" TWELVE gave him another squirt, "Ok, I am feeling fine now."

Ben Bigg glanced round. "Are we all here? Oh no, *where* is ONE? ONE, hurry up! Where are you?"

"Hello people, ONE here. What do you think of my new outfit?" ONE appeared at the door dressed in a white suit, embroidered with black threads and diamonds.

"Urrgh, far out man!" muttered SEVEN, who had just woken up.

ELEVEN rolled over and sat up with a start. "Wow!" he exclaimed. All the other numbers whistled and stamped their feet – "Super!" – "Great!" they yelled.

"Yes, very nice!" said TWO.

"Yes, very nice!" said THREE.

"Groovy!" said FOUR.

"How *could* you FOUR?" chorused TWO and THREE, annoyed that he'd not joined their chorus.

Ben Bigg walked over to ONE, "Now you have arrived at last, can we get on *please*? By the way, your white suit is very nice, but it will not stay clean very long. Right, places *please,* everyone." At this, all the numbers dashed to their correct positions on the clock face. Even NINE managed to get in the right place. "Now are we ready? TV on? Camera on?" called Ben Bigg.

A voice in the background then spoke, ".......and here is the nine o'clock news."

"Boing, boing, boing, boing, boing, boing, boing, boing boing," chimed Ben Bigg............

Story 16

The Land of the
Backwards People

Once upon a time, or as they would say in the Land of the Backwards People, '........*time a upon Once*'. Yes, amazingly everything there was backwards! Philip found this out very quickly. He was kicking his football about; he was the George Best of Baker Street. He kicked the ball, which hit a post and re-bounded so quickly that he did not have time to move out of the way. It bowled him over like a ninepin and he fell, hitting his head, which knocked him out.

"*?alright you Are*", (Are you alright?), said a voice and Philip felt a hand shake his shoulder. "*?alright you Are*", it said again. Philip slowly opened his eyes; oh crikey, his head really hurt and there was blood on his shirt. What had happened to him?

"*?feel you do How*", (How do you feel?), the voice said again.

Looking round, Philip began to make out things, even though they were a bit hazy. He tried to sit up.

"*!again bleed head your make will you or still stay, No*", (No, stay still or you will make your head bleed again!) and he felt a firm hand press down on his shoulder. Something must have happened to him because he could not understand what was being said, or who was saying it!

A vague, fuzzy shape stepped in front of him and said, "*now bleeding isn't cut the least At ?now feel you do how, Hello*" (Hello, how do you feel now? At least the cut isn't bleeding now).

Philip replied, "Pardon?" The vague, fuzzy shape became clearer and he could see that it was a young man dressed very much like himself, but he had completely blue hair! "I'm sorry but I do not know what you are saying; I cannot understand you. Who are you?"

"*.Eric me call can you, but Clark-Wilson de George Andrew David Philip am I, Hi*" (Hi, I am Philip David Andrew George de Wilson-Clark, but you can call me Eric). Eric knelt down and shook Philip by the hand. Now Philip, even though his head still hurt, suddenly realised why he could not understand the man called Eric – yes, he was talking backwards!

"Hi, I am Philip. I'm sorry I did not understand you before, but I did not realise you were talking backwards. Don't you find that awkward?" he asked.

A puzzled look came over Eric's face. "*?you do are you where know don't You .this like speak all We*" (We all speak like this. You don't know where you are do you?). He pointed to the village around them, saying, "*everything ,on so and backwards walk ,backwards eat ,backwards everything do always We .People Backwards the of Land the is This*". (This is the Land of the Backwards People. We always do everything backwards, eat backwards, walk backwards and so on, everything.)

Philip laughed, *ouch* that hurt his head, but it just seemed so funny! He looked at the people going by, and yes, they were all walking backwards! He looked at the clock on the church tower – even that was going backwards and the birds, well you've probably guessed it, they were flying backwards too! He put his hand to his head, "How did I get here?" he asked. "All I can remember was playing football, then I think I fell and hit my head."

"*?face your seen you have Actually .here you brought we so, mud the in down-face were you and screen Vector our on it saw we, Yes*" (Yes, we saw it on our Vector screen and you were face-down in the mud, so we brought you here. Actually, have you seen your face?). Eric put his hand into his pocket and bought out a shiny tin which he handed to Philip, "*Look*". (Look).

Philip looked and what a mess his face was; mud was everywhere – in his hair, up his nose and even in his ears! (That was not too good because it would mean he would have to wash his hair and his ears again, which he hated!) Suddenly he started to laugh. He rolled about on the ground clutching his stomach, laughing and laughing.

"*?Philip ,funny so is What*" (What is so funny, Philip?) asked Eric, but then he too started to smile, joining in the laughter. When Eric laughed his tummy wobbled and this made Philip laugh even more.

"Oh, oh!" he gasped. "I look so funny and silly. Just look at my face. At least it doesn't matter too much about my football gear because that always gets muddy."

Again Eric looked puzzled, "*?gear football and football is What*" (What is football and what is football gear?)

"Well, it's a game played by people in a team against another team. They kick a ball around a pitch and try to score a goal in the net of the opposite team at the other end of the pitch," explained Philip. "It lasts about one and half hours and whoever scores the most goals, wins!"

"*?it play to how me teach you Will .fun sounds That*", asked Eric (That sounds fun. Will you teach me how to play it?) "*.you as way same the speak don't we because though* *problem a have will We"* (We will have a problem though because we don't speak the same way as you.)

Philip thought this problem over and then he had a brilliant idea, (he had them every so often). "Have you got a very large, unbreakable safety mirror?" he asked.

".here it bring to someone get can I ,wait you If .Observatory the at mirror large a is there think I ,yes Um", mused Eric. (Um yes, I think there is a large mirror at the Observatory. If you wait, I can get someone to bring it here.) Eric stuck his finger into his left ear and closed his eyes. He seemed to make contact with someone. Suddenly, Philip saw more people, all walking backwards of course, and all dressed like Eric, but with different coloured hair. Between them they were carrying some enormous mirrors that glistened and shone in the sun.

"?Eric ,these want you do Where", they asked. (Where do you want these, Eric?) *"Philip ask better had You"*, answered Eric. (You had better ask Philip).

"Hi," said Philip. "Can you put them over there please?" pointing to the end of the field. They were carried very carefully and fixed securely to the wall. "That's great! Now, if you play football, by using the mirrors to *reverse* everything, you will be able to play it the same way we do at home – look!" He carefully put the ball on the ground in front of him, "See, you kick it like this between the posts and that is called scoring a goal!" He kicked it gently towards Eric. He then went on to explain some simple rules of football to the gathered crowd.

Eric then had a go, so did his friend and his friend's friends, then all the other people joined in. Philip then had *another* brilliant idea! "Eric, if you put mirrors all round the field, you can then play a proper game of football, the way we play it at home!"

"!idea good a What", said Eric, (What a good idea!) sending his friends to get as many mirrors as they could find. It did not take them long. Soon the grass field was surrounded

by reflected light. All the mirrors were safety mirrors as Philip had insisted. Ok, they were all ready to play. Well, every rule in the book was broken in the first ten minutes! But it was not too bad for a first attempt. Philip blew the final whistle and everyone crowded round, laughing and shaking his hand.

"*!game great a What*"

"*!toe sore a got I've*"

"*?again play we can When*" (What a great game! I've got a sore toe! When can we play again?)

Eric came over to Philip and put his hand on his arm, saying, "*!great was That .football of game the us teaching for you Thank .do you like just it play can we mirrors the using By*" (By using the mirrors we can play it just like you do. Thank you for teaching us the game of football. That was great!)

Philip laughed, slapping Eric on the back. "I'm *so* glad you enjoyed it. If you keep practising, we might be able to give you a game sometime. Now I really must go home, but I'm not sure how to get there."

"*!easy that It's .safe quite It's .home be will you and it through walk, end the at mirror the to Go*", answered Eric. (Go to the mirror at the end, walk through it and you will be home. It's quite safe. It's that easy!) "*Goodbye my friend.*"

Philip looked at Eric in amazement – had he heard him correctly? Eric had spoken and he sounded *exactly* like him! He shook his head. "Wow! I'm *so* glad I met you Eric! Keep practising the football and then maybe I will see you again. Goodbye!" Philip waved his hand to Eric, walked up to the mirror and suddenly, he found himself outside, *exactly* where he had been playing football earlier.

One thing was puzzling him though..... where was his football?

Story 17

The Lost Cloud

Emily, or 'Em' as she was known, was seven years old, but she was a tall girl for her age. She had just started at her new school and she was making lots of new friends. Her 'extra special' friend was Samantha, but Emily couldn't say Samantha, so she called her 'Sam'. A friendship was formed at Milton Infant School for Girls and Boys. Em and Sam went everywhere together. Each playtime they skipped or played hopscotch, but their favourite was 'kiss-chase'.

One lovely, warm day, Mrs Eden the headmistress, told the class that, as it was the last day of term tomorrow, they could bring in their favourite toy or game to play with. Both girls were very excited trying to decide what they would take in to school on Friday. "I think I will bring my doll that cries," said Em.

"My dolly wets the bed," replied Sam, "and if I bring her in she might wet my desk!" Both girls giggled at this thought.

"Well what are you going to bring in then?" asked Em, twiddling her hair through her fingers. (Em was very good at this – her fingers always managed to tie themselves up in knots).

Sam looked thoughtful, "Well, maybe I will bring in Dodo, my next bestest doll."

"What does she look like?" Emily asked.

"She's got curly hair like my mummy, but not the same colour, and blue eyes. My mummy has got brown eyes," Sam replied. These very important discussions went on for the rest of playtime and all the way home.

Friday, the last day of term, was another lovely warm, sunny day. Emily brought in her doll, all wrapped up in its lovely fluffy, white shawl, with a little pillow; whilst Sam had Dodo, her second bestest doll. They skipped ahead of their mothers but stopped at the gates to kiss them goodbye. Everyone was shouting and laughing in the school playground, showing their toys to each other. The bell rang for lessons, which went very quickly. Playtime in the warm sun came and went, then it was another lesson, then it was dinnertime; the girls' favourite time of day.

Emily and Sam both took their dolls out onto the grass at the back of the school and sat down. They laid the shawl and pillow on the grass, then put their dolls very carefully down on top of it. The warm sun made both girls start to feel very, very sleepy..... Suddenly, Sam poked Emily, saying, "Em look!" Emily looked and saw some white bits of fluff moving around their dolls which were lying on the shawl. Both girls sat up; what was it? The white, fluffy bits seemed to be trying to pick up the white shawl and were making funny, squeaking noises which sounded like birds in the trees. As they watched, the white, fluffy bits stopped and were suddenly quiet. A larger, white fluffy bit seemed to float over to where Emily and Sam were sitting, with their hands over their mouths and eyes as big as saucers.

The larger white, fluffy bit muttered, "We have a problem."

"Did it actually *speak*?" whispered Emily to Sam. "What did it say?"

At this, the larger white, fluffy bit repeated itself, "We seem to have a problem," settling slowly down onto the grass, near the girls.

Sam whispered, "Oh, you *do* speak! What...what are you?"

The white, fluffy bit rose a little off the grass, shook itself, spun round and floated back down.

"*I* am a cloud! And we appear to have lost one of our cloud group. We think that you have got it wrapped around one of your dolls."

Sam leaned closer to Emily and whispered, "They think your white, fluffy shawl is their lost cloud."

Emily giggled, "Don't be daft!"

"Yes they do!" insisted Sam.

Emily turned to the cloud and pointed to her doll's white, fluffy shawl and said, "That is *not* your cloud. That is a shawl for wrapping things in. It is made of wool and my grandma made it for me."

The larger, fluffy cloud looked puzzled, (if you can imagine what a puzzled, fluffy cloud could look like!) It seemed to shake itself, "Oh dear, we seem to have made a big mistake. We saw your white, fluffy shawl as we were floating by and from up there, it looked just like the cloud we seem to have lost somewhere."

"How can you lose a cloud?" asked Sam.

"The Great Wind came and just blew it away," replied the large cloud. "It went high up into the air. We could not keep up with it, so now we have lost it." Emily looked across at the other clouds, all white and fluffy, sitting on her shawl. Suddenly she had an idea and whispered in Sam's ear.... Sam nodded.

Emily said to the large cloud, "I have got some white, fluffy cotton-wool in my dolly's pillow, you could have that. It is very like a cloud. Would that do? My grandma would refill my dolly's pillow for me."

All the other clouds started twittering to each other and the large, fluffy cloud twittered back. "That sounds very nice," it said. "Can we see it please?" Emily picked up her doll's pillow and took out the soft, white cotton-wool, laying it carefully on the ground near the large cloud.

The large cloud seemed to 'feel' the cotton wool, "Mmm, very nice, so very soft... Yes, it will be just right. Thank you so very much, we will take it with us."

Suddenly, Emily and Sam heard the bell ringing for the end of dinnertime. They must have been dreaming! They bent down to pick up their dolls. Emily was puzzled though – her doll's pillow was empty! It did not have any cotton-wool inside. She didn't know why.

Sam said to Emily, "I had a very strange dream about a lost cloud and cotton-wool or something."

"Yes, so did *I*!" answered Emily. They started to compare their strange dreams. Could that explain the empty pillow?

As they walked back into school, Emily looked up at the blue sky, the warm sun, and the white, fluffy clouds...... She wondered if it had really happened?

Story 18

Little Bing and Big Bong

BING and BONG were the bells at the local church. Every Sunday they rang out – 'bing-bong, bing-bong', reminding the villagers that it was time to go to church. Mikey and John were in the church choir and had to get there a bit earlier than the rest of their families.

This particular Sunday morning started off like any other. It was warm and sunny. Both boys set off early for church. Tell the truth, they did go a little bit earlier because they wanted to look at the new Zero car in the window of the garage in the High Street. "Wow, what a machine!" breathed John, his nose pressed against the window.

"Yes, I bet it goes over the ton!" replied Mikey. "I would *love* to have a ride in it, wouldn't you?"

John nodded, "Yeh, too right. Bet it goes so fast no-one would ever catch up with it." Both boys stood looking at the beautiful, red car with silver wheels and headlights the size of dinner plates. They turned towards the church, vowing that, 'one day we will have a ride in it'.

They neared the church, but something appeared to be wrong – there were no bells ringing out. This was very strange!

The boys hurried into the church and went into the vestry, but there was no-one in there. "The vicar must be up in the belfry," said Mikey. "Come on, let's go and find him." John pushed open the door to the tower and the boys started to climb the spiral stairway up to the belfry. The tower was very tall and the bells were about half way up, in a special room. This was the room where the bell ringers 'pulled' the ropes to make the bells ring. There were six bells in the tower and they sounded lovely when they were all being rung.

John and Mikey puffed their way up, up and round, into the little room. What a sight met their eyes! Mr Glover, their Vicar, lay on the floor, not moving.

"Is he dead?" whispered Mikey.

"I don't know," replied John, as both boys went over to the Vicar.

Mr. Glover opened his eyes as they knelt down beside him. "Oh, thank goodness you have come!" said Mr. Glover breathlessly. "I have fallen and hurt my leg, but could not get back down the stairs to get help. I think it is broken because I cannot move it. Can you go and fetch help for me, please?"

John nodded, "Ok, but we had better put this coat over you to keep you warm."

Mikey brought the coat over and they carefully placed it over Mr. Glover. "It's a long way back to the town," he said. "Is there a way we can get help more quickly?"

Both boys then thought. Suddenly, John punched the air! "I've got it! I know how we can get help – Bing and Bong!"

"What, you mean the two bells?" queried Mikey.

"Yes. If we can pull them so they sound wrong, someone will be bound to come and investigate," John quickly replied.

"It's a brilliant idea, let's go!" called Mikey, starting to untie the bell ropes for Bing and Bong.

The boys turned to Mr. Glover who was still lying down, his face was very pale and he seemed to be in a lot of pain now. They explained what their plan was and Mr. Glover managed to nod in agreement, then put his fingers in his ears!

They began to pull on the ropes. Once the bells began to move the two boys pulled as hard as they could. The noise was *deafening* – 'clang bang, clang bang, crash' – it sounded awful! Still the boys bravely pulled on the ropes and the noise went on and on! *Surely* someone must hear Bing and Bong making this terrible sound?

Suddenly there was a movement at the tower door and PC Davis came panting in. "Good heavens, what is this awful noise and what are you two boys doing?" he shouted, signalling to Mikey and John to stop ringing the bells. Slowly, the bells became quiet, so the boys could explain that Mr. Glover appeared to have a broken leg and he couldn't move, and he also had a lot of pain. Mr. Glover took his fingers out of his ears now it had become quieter. The boys explained that the only way they think of to get help was to ring the bells, rather badly!

"Well, you did that alright!" said PC Davis. He turned to Mr. Glover saying, "Right Eric, let's have a look at you now." He very gently helped Mr. Glover move himself into a more comfortable position. "Mmm, that does look like it might be broken. I will ring for an ambulance, so we can get you to hospital." PC Davis spoke into his radio whilst John and Mikey watched.

Within a few minutes the boys could hear a siren and went over to the window. They could see the ambulance coming down the road with its blue lights flashing. Then, when it stopped outside the church gates, two men got out carrying a special folding chair and a big first-aid kit. They walked up the path and disappeared inside the church.

A few minutes, no, *quite* a few minutes later, the two men arrived in the doorway, puffing and a bit red in the face, "Crikey, what a climb!" PC Davis waited until the men had got their breath, then explained the situation and how John and Mikey had saved the Vicar's life.

Mr. Glover agreed with him as the ambulance men started to check him out. "They did very well. If it had not been for their quick thinking, I do not know how long I would have been here."

The two ambulance men put a sort of puffy bag round Mr. Glover's leg, just to be on the safe side in case it was broken and gave him some pain relief. This meant they could move him very gently into the folding chair.

"This will be fun, getting downstairs again!" remarked one of them.

"Stop, just a minute please," said Mr Glover. "I just want to really thank you two boys for what you did, and once I am better, I want to reward you properly." Mikey and John beamed at each other.

Thus it was, that two out-of-breath ambulance men with their patient, the local policeman and two boys, carefully made their way down the spiral staircase and out to the waiting ambulance. Mr. Glover gave the boys a 'thumbs up' sign.....

Now can anyone guess what happened to our two heroes a few days later? The story of how they had helped save the Vicar's life appeared in the local paper, but it was a knock at the door when the boys were playing on John's computer, that amazed them both! John's father opened the door.....

Outside, stood a gentleman in a grey chauffeur's uniform with a peaked cap and behind him....... was a beautiful, red car – the Zero! The chauffeur explained to John's father that he was instructed to speak to the two local heroes and John's father called the boys downstairs. "This gentleman wishes to speak with you two."

"John, Mikey, I am very pleased to meet you both. My name is Graham and I am here on behalf of Mr. Glover. He said he wanted to thank you for saving his life the other day and got in touch with your parents to ask if there was anything really special you would both like." Graham paused, then continued, "Apparently your dream is to go for a ride in the new Zero car? Well, now you can and your father can fill the spare seat!"

The two boys could not believe their eyes, or ears – did they hear him correctly – they were actually going for a ride in THAT car? Wow!! A few seconds later, two very proud boys and one very proud father, made their way out to the big, red car. Graham opened the doors with a 'magic' key and they all got in. The car slowly purred away from the kerb and, as the boys leaned back in the black leather seats, John and Mikey secretly hoped that they would see some of their school mates............!

Story 19

The Melting Village

What a mess there was – everywhere was covered with melting chocolate!

The trees were brown shapes in brown, chocolate fields. The cars could not move because of the chocolate on the road, well, if you could see the road that is! People kept losing their shoes in the brown, sticky mess.

The little people who lived there could not understand it. They had never done anything wrong – they had paid their taxes when they were due, so why was Mindoan the Sun God, doing this to them? Tandor, the son of Tomis the baker, was busy trying to sweep the sticky chocolate mess out of his garden. The awful mess was all that was left of his house – a large, brown, sticky heap – (mind you, it did taste nice!) Next door Dympna, the jeweller, was trying to sort out his clocks and jewellery from the big blobs of chocolate that had been his shop. He was crying, "What shall I do? I am ruined!"

"It's terrible isn't it?" said Tandor. "Why has Mindoan done this? He must have become so hot and cross that he has melted our village into nothing. The only place that is almost left standing is Jondo's freezer shop. Gosh, I wonder if we can do anything about this mess?" as he picked out a necklace from the melted shop.

"There's nothing we can do," muttered Dympna, as a blob of hot chocolate dripped down onto his shoe.

He paused, "No, wait a minute, maybe we *can* do something! If someone could go and talk to Mindoan, perhaps he would cool things down a wee bit?"

"That's a good idea," agreed Tomis, "who can we send?"

"Well, I can't go, I'm too old!" muttered Dympna, holding his back as if he had suddenly become very old.

"Ok, it looks as if it will have to be me then," Tandor replied, putting his broom down. It immediately fell over into the heap of sticky chocolate that he had already swept up. "I will go and see what can be done." Tandor felt in his pocket to see that his magic coin was still there. His grandfather had given it to Tandor many, many years ago, and grandfather had been given the coin by an old gypsy, who said that it would bring him good luck. The magic was in the coin, if you just wished long and hard enough whilst holding it. Tandor never went anywhere without it.

Off he went whistling to himself. He crossed the river at the bottom of the village which was full of melting, chocolate lumps, floating like brown icebergs on the water. On and on walked Tandor, passing lots of people who were trying their best to clean up where their homes had been.

He came to the crossroads where the signs pointed one way to the village, another to Windy Valley, the third pointed to Darkness Woods and the fourth to the Land of Mindoan. This was the road he wanted! It was a fairly long walk and Tandor was beginning to feel very tired. "I must rest for a moment," he thought and, as he rested, his fingers touched the coin in his pocket. "I wonder.... I wonder if it really *does* work magic?" Tandor grasped the coin in his fingers, making his wish, "I wish to visit the Sun God Mindoan..." As he thought that, there was a sudden flash of light! Instantly, he found himself standing in a very, very bright room. "Where am I?" he wondered out loud.

"This is the Palace of Mindoan, the Sun God. What are you doing here? Where did you come from? You do not live in this city! Do you have an appointment?" questioned a cheery-looking little man who appeared at Tandor's side. He was dressed in yellow; every shade of yellow you could imagine. The strange thing was, he gave off a sort of warmth, like the heat from a fire.

"My name is Tandor, what's yours?" asked Tandor, holding out his hand.

"Oh, I am Obis, Mindoan's chancellor. May I ask why you have come to our beautiful city?" he replied, shaking Tandor's hand.

"Well, I've come to ask the Sun God, Mindoan, not to shine quite so hotly because it is melting my village, which is made of chocolate," answered Tandor.

"Oh gosh! I'm so sorry," said Obis, "but I must admit we have had a few problems with our heating system lately, and we did not realise that people would suffer, especially those living so far away."

"Please can I speak with Mindoan?" pleaded Tandor.

"Yes of course you may. Follow me," and Obis beckoned Tandor to follow him. Off they went. Tandor had never seen so much light, or felt so hot and sticky! He longed for a cool drink. At long last they arrived at the palace and entered a beautiful room. A majestic-looking man was pacing up and down, wringing his hands. He, too, was dressed in yellow, but he had a crown on his head and jewels everywhere.

"So, this must be Mindoan," Tandor thought. He stood in awe as 'flames' and 'heat' seemed to leap from the Sun God's robes. They shimmered and danced in the air. Obis bowed low, "Excuse me Sire, this is Tandor who urgently requests an audience with you."

The Sun God beckoned, "Come close Tandor. What is your problem?"

Tandor bowed respectfully saying, "Your Majesty, the sun is making things too hot in our village, causing our houses and shops to melt. You see, our village is made of chocolate. Would it be possible to turn down the heat a little bit, Sire?"

Mindoan sighed, "I'm terribly sorry about this. I assure you that it is not intentional. Something has gone wrong with our heating controls and no-one seems able to fix it. Do you happen to know anything about machinery?"

"Well, yes I know a little bit because I do help my father in his bakery and I do look after his machines," answered Tandor.

"Would it be possible for you to take a look at ours?" asked Mindoan.

Tandor nodded, "Yes, I certainly will. Where is it?"

"Over here," said Mindoan, going over to an elaborate door and opening it. Beyond were machines and dials of different shapes and sizes. "It appears to have a fault here," Mindoan announced, pointing to one piece of machinery, which was coughing and spluttering loudly.

Tandor looked at the machine. "Oh yes, your flugel damper control is jammed open!" he grinned, reaching down into the centre of the machine and fiddling with the dials and levers. "Have you any grease?" inquired Tandor. At once Obis appeared, with a huge, green tub. "There, that should fix it! This control knob needs constant greasing so that it doesn't stick open."

"Thank you so very much!" said Mindoan, clasping Tandor's hand. "How can we repay you? I will of course now be able to turn down the heat over your village, so I do hope you will be able to rebuild your houses."

"Yes, we *will* be able to rebuild the village, once the chocolate sets again, but would it be possible to have a lovely, cold drink please, as I have never felt so hot!" asked Tandor.

Mindoan clapped his hands and a servant appeared at his side, carrying a gold cup full of an ice-cold liquid. "Here you are my friend, please drink." Tandor sipped the sweet, cold drink; it was delicious and cooling.

When he had finished, Mindoan said, "Obis, would you please take Tandor to the astral lift so he may return home?" Turning to Tandor, he extended his hand saying, "Thank you again my friend. I am sure you will find things a lot cooler now."

Tandor shook the King's hand which now felt cool and quite bearable to touch. "Goodbye your Majesty," he said bowing low, "and thank you."

"Come Tandor," called Obis from the doorway, as Tandor slowly backed out of the room. They went down a passage, stopping outside another door. "This is the astral lift. It will take you exactly to your home. Good luck!" Tandor stepped inside what appeared to be an ordinary lift. Obis pressed a button and 'whoosh', in a split second, Tandor found himself again standing in the sticky mess of chocolate that had been his house. But it *did* feel cooler.....

"Hi Dympna," called Tandor. "I have spoken to Mindoan and managed to get the heat turned down. They were having trouble with their heating system, which I was able to fix for them. Yes, it really does feel cooler here now."

"Yes, you did very well Tandor, the whole village thanks you," replied Dympna. "All we have to do now is rebuild these lumps of chocolate. Mmm, I think I will build a different-shaped shop, with even bigger windows!" He set to work busily shaping the already-solidifying chocolate into bricks for building.

Tandor watched thoughtfully, "I am going to build a palace like Mindoan's, with a bakery in the grounds," he announced. He, too, started to shape bricks from the chocolate, but he kept nibbling at them!

"You won't have enough for your palace if you keep eating it!" laughed Dympna, *his* face and hands all covered in sticky chocolate!

"Oh well, maybe I will have to make it slightly smaller then!" smiled Tandor, licking his lips.

Story 20

Leslie the Leaf Man
and Whispers of the Leaves

'Whoosh, whoosh, whoosh', – the wind rustled the leaves on the tree, making them dance and sway about. Every now and again the leaves would become loose and float gently down to the ground. It was that time of the year known as Autumn. Summer had finished and Winter was not quite ready to appear.

The leaves made a brightly-coloured carpet on the ground – reds and yellows, browns and greens. They were so beautiful, just like Nature's jewels lying carelessly tossed onto a piece of green velvet.

Debbie was walking through these beautiful leaves in the park, watching her mother push her baby brother on the swings. "Mummy, where do the new, green leaves come from for next year?" she called to her mother.

"I don't really know Debs," replied her mother. "We will have to look in a book when we get home to find the answer." Debbie sat down on the end of one of the long, wooden benches, day-dreaming, swinging her feet back and forth through the leaves.

"Sssh!" Debbie looked round. "Ssssh! Up here, look up!" said a voice. Debbie looked up and saw a green figure sitting on a branch. "No, don't be afraid, I'm not going to hurt you. I'm Leslie the Leaf Man."

Debbie looked across to where her mother was still pushing her brother on the swings. Turning back to the little figure she said, "Leslie the Leaf Man, what is that?"

"Well, I heard you asking your mother about the new, green leaves that come out in the Spring, so I thought I would quickly show you where they are. You must not make a noise or you will wake them up too soon," answered Leslie. "They are asleep."

"Asleep? How can leaves be asleep?" asked Debbie, unsure about this.

The Leaf Man pointed to all the lovely leaves that were floating down. "You see all these leaves?" Debbie nodded. "Well these leaves are now dying." Debbie nodded again. The Leaf Man continued, "Leaves grow in the Spring, and during the Summer they provide shelter and food for all sorts of animals and creatures, and the birds build nests in the leafy bushes. Then, when Autumn arrives, they gradually fade away again. The foods and minerals they needed to live on are reduced and saved for the new leaves. These are now growing within the trees. Look!" The Leaf Man beckoned Debbie over to an old tree behind the bench, "Look, this is the leaf nursery."

Debbie paused, she could see her mother was sitting on a seat watching her brother play on the slide. The old tree was just behind the bench, so she could not resist a quick peep up into the branches. The branches were bare and brown and she thought they looked a bit like a skeleton rattling about in the breeze. Anyway, she looked inside and saw what appeared to be tightly-rolled, green bundles. Above each bundle was a tube, dripping some clear liquid. Leslie the Leaf Man said very quietly, "This is the Leaf Nursery where all your new leaves grow, ready to come out on the trees next Spring."

Standing there in silence, Debbie thought, "What's the stuff dripping down? Is that their food?"

"Yes, that's right," replied Leslie, obviously reading her mind! "They take it in very slowly during the Winter and then in the Spring they are able to burst out and grow into the lovely, green leaves and trees you see around you." He swept his arm round in a circle, pointing to the trees that lined the park.

"Um, how did you know I was thinking that?" asked Debbie.

The Leaf Man closed his eyes, whispering, "Magic!" With that, he suddenly disappeared!

"Debs, come along, we must be getting home now as it's nearly tea-time," called her mother.

"Mummy, did you see him?" asked Debbie.

"Did I see who?"

"Leslie the Leaf Man! He was all green and he showed me the leaf nursery in that tree over there," Debbie pointed across to the old tree behind the bench.

Her mother desperately tried to keep a straight face, saying, "Debs darling, you have been dozing on that seat for far too long! There has not been anyone else here all afternoon except you, me and your brother and certainly no-one dressed in green!" Debbie now was puzzled; she was *sure* she had been and looked in the old tree, hadn't she? Right, she would go and have *another* look now!

"Mummy, please come with me and I will show you the leaf nursery in that old tree," taking hold of her mother's hand.

"Alright darling, I'm coming," replied her mother, scooping up her brother and putting him into his pushchair. Together they went round to the old tree and looked up inside. At first, Debbie could not see anything, but, looking closer she saw some soft, silky rolls, shaped like little sausages. She put her finger to her lips, "Sssh! See mummy, there they all are, fast asleep, just like Leslie the Leaf Man told me. Then when they are ready in the Spring, they will wake up and make the trees and bushes green again."

Her mother nodded wisely. Maybe she did not believe in fairies because all she could see were spider webs and silk cocoons, spun by the caterpillars she knew lived in the tree.....

"Oh, for the wonderful imagination of children!" she mused.

Story 21

The Clock

It was dinnertime in the year 2000. The Clock should have struck 12 noon – what had happened?

Val glanced at her watch. Yes, it certainly said noon. "I suppose someone has forgotten to replace the batteries in The Clock again," she said, to no-one in particular.

"Pardon?" said Pippa. "I presume they have not *wound* The Clock after the holidays!" she added, realising it was Valerie who had first spoken.

"Oh, does it need winding then? I thought it ran on batteries or something; most things do nowadays!" repeated Valerie. "Fancy that, you actually wind it up!" Valerie sniffed delicately.

Now, Valerie was the office snob! Everything she had was either electrical, computerised, or operated by someone else! She had a 'showhouse' home with every possible gadget: a dishwasher, electric tin opener and even an electric tooth-brush! Yet to Val, anything mechanical was a complete mystery, so understanding the office clock, (or to be more precise The Old Clock), was beyond her. Pippa smiled to herself, "Dear Val, she would be totally lost if her all-electric home suffered a power cut.....!"

Suddenly The Clock in question gave a shudder. Pippa looked at it quickly – gosh, it seemed to be going backwards? She looked again – yes, it *was* going backwards! She looked across at Val who was busy polishing her bright red nails and fiddling with her mobile phone. Pippa decided not to say anything to her because Val would think she was stupid. Standing up, she announced, "Am just popping down to David's office for a moment Val, I won't be a tick." With that, she went out of the office and down the corridor, knocking lightly on his office door.

In David's office, Pippa stood looking out of the window, trying to compose herself. Yes, The Clock *had* been going backwards. Gosh, did that mean that anything electrical would now become manual or mechanical? She shuddered. How would they cope? It would be just like when she joined the firm forty-five years ago.....

Pippa suddenly found herself in 1955.....

David's computer no longer sat on his desk; no longer existed! In its place was an inkstand, with pens and pencils. Nearby was a pile of notepaper and envelopes. What had happened to her? Slowly Pippa looked round the office, taking in the changes that seemed to have somehow taken place. She looked at her clothes, had they changed as well? No, thank goodness, they were still the same: pretty summer dress, white sandals and her favourite necklace. Pippa stared out of the window, yes things outside looked to be normal. The traffic was still going along the road; people were still hurrying about, shopping. Standing there, Pippa shook her head, "How strange," she thought.

Quietly, she turned to leave David's office, peering out into the corridor. What would she see she wondered? At first the corridor looked normal, but suddenly she realised that the coffee machine which normally stood outside the door, had vanished! A dent in the carpet was the only thing that indicated it had ever stood there. Slowly, walking towards to her office she could hear a commotion coming from within. Opening the door, revealed..... she was not sure..... an amazing sight greeted her!

Val was standing there, screaming, with tears pouring down her face! Pauline and some of the other girls were trying to calm her down, but the looks on their faces said it all – what had happened? Pippa now saw a totally different office from the one she had left minutes earlier.

Gone were the computers; gone was the big photocopier in the corner; gone was the special machine which recorded information for their computers; gone were all the latest telephones; gone were the remote controls for the air-conditioning and central heating units! In their places had appeared some large, black, manual typewriters, a hand operated photocopier machine, black telephones and tightly-closed windows.

Val was still screaming, "My mobile has vanished! Where is my computer? What on *earth* is that black thing?" pointing to the telephone.

Pauline turned to Pippa, "Do you have any idea what has just happened here? We were all working at our desks and all of a sudden a sort of whirlwind blew through the office, swirled round, and when it stopped, this is what had happened!" – indicating the chaos. Pippa slowly shook her head, but found her gaze drawn to The Clock, the one that had appeared to be going backwards.

Amazingly, the Clock was still going backwards – time was in reverse! Pauline looked across to where Pippa was staring at The Clock; she couldn't believe her eyes either! She hissed, "Well any bright ideas Pip?"

Pippa inclined her head a bit, then glanced across at Val, who by now seemed to have stopped screaming, although her face was all red and blotchy from crying. "Yes, but I will need your help."

"Ok."

"Right Pauline, can you find The Clock key and the set of steps please?" Pauline hurried off to find them.

Pippa went across to Val and tried to explain that this thing that had happened, appeared to be a 'timewarp' because of all the electrical disturbances in the room.

"But I can't be without my gadgets!" wailed Val. "What will I do without my mobile phone, my I-pad, my computer?"

Pippa ignored all this. "This 'timewarp' happened, just to show us how different life used to be back in a 1950's office. It started when you complained about having to wind The Clock. That Clock is part of history and should be treated with respect. These gadgets," and she pointed to the old manual typewriters and the hand-operated copier, "were what our parents used back then. Things were not electrical; it was proper work. I suppose this is a weird way to make us respect the past and appreciate the future." Val nodded unconvincingly, glancing round at her colleagues who were in agreement.

At this moment, Pauline came back into the office, clutching the steps and a large, brass key. "Got it!" she cried, waving it in the air.

Val asked Pippa, "Just *what* are you proposing to do now?" continuing to sniff into her tissues.

"Well I guess that if we stop the clock, then rewind it fully, this 'timewarp' will vanish! Unless anyone else has any other bright ideas?"

No-one had, so Pauline put the steps by the side of The Clock, giving the brass key to Pippa, "Over to you Pip."

Pippa took the key, "Well, here goes!" Climbing the steps, she opened the glass front of The Clock, and grasped the hands firmly together. She moved both hands round to 12 o'clock, inserted the key and started to wind it. Slowly, slowly she wound it, and when it would not go any further she released the two hands. Everyone in the office was now watching with bated breath – even Val had stopped sniffing!

Very slowly, the hands started to move as twelve chimes began to ring out. "Y-e-e-s-s! Well done Pip!" as a round of applause ran through the office.

"Gosh look, our computers are back!" called a voice. The girls looked round the office and everything seemed to be 'back to normal' – the computers were back, modern phones, the photocopiers were all back in their proper places. Where had all the 1950's equipment gone? Why did it happen? All these questions but no answers.

Val turned to her colleagues, "I'm so *very* sorry girls, but it might have been something to do with my obsession with gadgets. I promise I will leave them at home from now on, but I still need my mobile phone, in case of emergency, you understand!"

Pauline and Pippa smiled at her, saying in unison, "Yes, we'll believe it when we see it!" and they all laughed.

"Tell you what, does anyone fancy a coffee?" called a little voice from the back of the office.

"What a brilliant idea!" replied Pippa, as they all trailed out into the corridor, where the coffee machine should be. She crossed her fingers, hoping that it too had also come back. Yes, it was back! She breathed a big sigh of relief, smiling to herself.

Pauline heard her sharp intake of breath and leaned over saying, "Well done Pip, well done!"

Story 22

The Paper Steps

The steps looked beautiful; all white and smooth with a glorious sparkle in them. They stretched up and up towards the Pearl Palace which stood tall and proud at the top of the hill. The Pearl Palace was the home of the Prince and Princess Gallanti. They had inherited it upon the sad deaths of the King and Queen. The sun shone on the hundreds of pretty palace windows, making them look like diamonds, set in sheets of pearl. The only thing that was causing a big headache for the Royal family were the steps. Yes, those same smooth, white steps with the sparkle in them. The problem? Well they were actually made of paper – yes, honestly! When anyone walked on them they would wrinkle and shred, which meant they needed to be replaced every day.

One day the Prince and Princess made a Proclamation saying, 'By Royal Decree, a Person is Needed to Assist the Royal Carpenter/Stonemason, to Solve the Problem of the Paper Steps'. Because a state visit abroad was due to take place immediately, the Prince and Princess agreed that the new staircase could be repaired during their absence.

Well, hundreds, nay thousands of people applied for the job, but the Lord Chamberlain and the Royal Carpenter/Stonemason chose a young man called Ericus Barneyboots-Smythe, but called 'Eric' for short, by his family and friends. Eric lived in a modest house in the town with his parents, brother and sister. He had studied carpentry and bricklaying, being taught by his father and grandfather, who had in turn, been taught by their fathers and grandfathers. Eric's skills were fantastic but now they would be tested to the limit!

The 'big morning' dawned, warm and sunny. Eric made his way to the Palace and met up with the Royal Carpenter/Stonemason in the palace gardens. They walked round to the 'paper steps' and stood looking at them. "Well, have you any fantastic ideas young man?" asked the Royal Carpenter/Stonemason.

"Yes, I do," replied Eric, taking some small pieces of marble from his pocket. "I have had these stored away since my grandfather discovered them in the hills many, many years ago. The large slabs are in my workshop. I can fit them beneath the 'paper steps' which I can use as a pattern, then carve them into identical new steps for the Prince and Princess."

The Royal Carpenter/Stonemason nodded, "Why hadn't I thought of that?" he said shrugging his shoulders and sighing deeply.

Eric, with the Royal Carpenter/Stonemason, called on the strongest men of the town to help lift the slabs of marble from his store and place them under the 'paper steps'. Then the long job of carving each individual step began. Day after day he toiled on them, chipping away until he got a flat, level surface, smoothing away any bumps, then finishing them off to a beautiful, shiny surface. He also put the royal coat-of-arms on the side of every step. At last the steps were finished! He announced to the Royal Carpenter/Stonemason that they were ready to be unveiled to the Prince and Princess upon their return.

The unveiling day arrived, again warm sun shone on the Pearl Palace. Trumpeters announced the arrival of the Royal couple, who walked round into the palace gardens and stood alongside the Royal Carpenter/Stonemason. All they could see were the 'paper steps', apparently still in place, stretching up towards the palace. Eric stepped forward, bowing low to the Royal couple. "Would Your Majesties like to walk up the 'paper steps' with me?" he asked, bowing low again. They nodded. Looking puzzled, they stepped forward onto the first step, onto the second step, onto the third one, then they stepped back down onto the lawn in amazement!

"Tell me Ericus, how have you managed to turn 'paper steps' into something solid?"

Again Eric bowed, "Allow me to show you Sire." With that, he signalled to the two lines of people who had been standing quietly by the sides of the steps. Very gently they slid the 'paper steps' off, revealing a beautiful flight of white, marble steps, glistening in the sunlight, all engraved with the royal coat-of-arms. "That is how I achieved it Sire." Eric slowly walked a little way up the new steps to show the royal couple that they were now perfectly safe to walk on.

"Bravo, how wonderful!" cried the Princess, clapping her hands. "How beautiful they look. Let us go up them, my Prince." The Prince nodded as the royal couple started walking up the steps. At the top, they turned to wave to their loyal subjects gathered below and at the same time beckoned Eric, the Royal Carpenter/Stonemason and the Lord Chamberlain to come up as well.

Eric slowly walked up the new steps bowing low to the royal couple. The Prince then spoke, "Ericus, you have completed a wonderful job here; the Princess and I would like to reward you." At this he turned to his wife, the Princess, who in turn beckoned the Royal Carpenter/Stonemason to come over. The Prince continued, "Our Royal Carpenter/

Stonemason is retiring next week so we would like to offer you his position within the Royal Court. Would you do us the honour of accepting this position?"

Looking astonished, Eric could not speak at first, then murmured, "Yes Sire, I would consider it a great honour to accept." He looked across at the Royal Carpenter/Stonemason, who stepped forward to place the Seal of Office round Eric's neck.

"Good luck young man!" he whispered in Eric's ear.

"Thank you!" answered Eric.

One very-delighted young man *nearly* jumped for joy, but then remembered where he was!

Story 23

The Lost Letters

"Lost letters!" boomed the man in charge of the Post Office, Mr. Philip Wilson. "Lost letters! Well, I don't have a clue where they go, but they must go somewhere." Janice Treadworthy and her daughter Jenny were in the little village post office on a hot, sunny July day. They had been expecting a Very Special Letter from Alec Treadworthy, who was away on some secret business. He was Janice's husband and adoring father of Jenny. Poor Jenny, her face fell. "Daddy said he would write, he promised me faithfully that I would get letters. He's been gone ages and ages now. Why hasn't he written?"

Mr. Philip Wilson came round the post office counter and knelt down by Jenny. "Hey Jen, don't be too upset. Your daddy has written to you I'm sure, but sometimes mysterious things happen to letters." He continued, "I expect they are all in a sack in the collection depot waiting to be sent to you. I will see what I can do." Mrs. Treadworthy smiled at Mr. Wilson, as he winked, "Leave it with me Jen."

After they left the Post Office, as it was early-closing day, Philip Wilson turned the 'OPEN' sign round to 'CLOSED', then locked up. He was thirsty because it had been a hot morning. Picking up his hat, he straightened the rim and put it on his head. It was a Homburg hat which had belonged to his grandfather.

Philip Wilson stepped outside into the hot sun. He turned right as he usually did, stopping at the corner shop to buy a bottle of ice-cold water. Slowly drinking from it, he absent-mindedly went into the alleyway that led the park and lake. Suddenly, he realised there was no park; instead he found himself in front of what appeared to be bags and bags of mail. He rubbed his eyes, yes they certainly were mail bags, probably full of letters, but what the heck were they doing here? Going over to one of the bags, he carefully opened it. Inside he saw hundreds of different-sized, different-coloured envelopes. As he looked, he became aware of something or someone standing quietly behind him. Philip turned round slowly and saw a man, who looked very familiar!

It suddenly dawned on him – this man was Alec Treadworthy, Jenny's dad and Janice's husband! Alec held out his hand saying, "Good to see you Philip."

Philip shook Alec's hand, "Likewise. How are you?" When he looked hard at Alec, he got a strange feeling but he did not know why.

Alec nodded, "I'm fine... yes fine... just fine."

Philip stared at Alec; there seemed to be something very different about him. "Are you *really* alright?" he asked.

"Yes really, but could you do something for me please, Philip?"

Philip nodded, "I can try. What do you want me to do?"

Alec stepped closer, "Actually," he whispered, " ..... I am dead! I have been dead about three months but my body has never been found. I had written some letters to Jenny and my Janice just before the 'accident', but they never got posted. I have them with me." Taking out some envelopes, he held them out to Philip, "Please will you deliver them for me and tell them I am fine."

Philip's hand shook as he took the letters, "What happened Alec?"

"There was an explosion aboard the submarine. It happened so fast that no-one survived and the Authorities don't even know where to start looking."

"Oh crikey!" was all Philip could say at first. "Yes, of course I will deliver them for you. Can I do anything else for you?"

Alec shook his head, "No thank you. Just tell them it happened so fast, but we are all fine now, just fine." As he said this, he appeared to 'fade away'. Philip looked at the letters still clasped in his hand. They were addressed to Janice and Jenny. He wondered how he could best deliver them, as Alec had asked. Should he say anything about what he knew?

Philip paused, and then made his decision.....

He went across to the sacks of mail, slipped the letters into the opened sack, closed it and noted the sack number '2713'. "I will look out for you '2713'!" he vowed. Turning round he found he was back in the alley; how that had happened – he had no idea! His hat was still on his head, he still had the half-finished bottle of water in his hand. Philip quickened his steps, back up the alleyway and round towards the corner shop; everything was normal.

Walking back into the Post Office, he realised the sacks had been delivered. When he looked at them, he saw sack number '2713' – yes, THE sack was there! Carefully, he opened it and, lying on top of all the other mail inside, were the ones Alec had given him. They were messy, almost as if they had been in water! Why hadn't he noticed this before?

He carefully took them out. Yes, they *were* the same envelopes. Putting them aside, he sorted out the rest of the mail into piles ready for delivery. Then, going across to the telephone, he dialled Janice Treadworthy's telephone number. "Hello Janice, Philip here. The 'lost letter' department have found some letters addressed to you and Jenny. I believe they could be the ones you were asking me about earlier today. I will keep them safe for you until you can come in to collect them."

Gently, he replaced the receiver. "Well Alec, I've delivered them as you asked." Very carefully he placed the letters on the shelf marked 'Lost/Returned Letters'. A sudden shiver went down Philip's back, as a cool puff of air entered the Post Office, which was strange, because the door was closed!

A ghost maybe?

Story 24

Swallowed Up By....?

"Yeh, whatever!" yelled Sophie, as she ran upstairs into her bedroom. Her mother, Ruth, watched as her ten, (going on twenty) year-old daughter ran up the stairs. She heard the bedroom door slam.

Ruth sighed – "Kids....! Phones.....! Arguments.....!"

Slamming her bedroom door, Sophie picked up her mobile phone, the cause of so many arguments, which was lying on her bed. She wanted to speak to her best friend, Angela, as she did dozens of times a day. Dialling Angela's number, Sophie noticed her phone heating up! It grew warmer and warmer until she dropped it quickly back onto her bed. What was happening to it? Sophie watched in amazement as her mobile phone began to grow 'bigger', disappearing into a cloud of 'blue smoke'.

Jumping up she ran to her bedroom door; crikey, it wouldn't open! "Help mum!" yelled Sophie, but there was no answer. Looking over her shoulder, she saw the 'blue smoke' was beginning to fill her bedroom. She ran across to the window and tried to open it, to let the smoke out, but it wouldn't open either! What was happening? Sophie was starting to panic.....

But, just as suddenly as the 'blue smoke' had appeared, it started to clear. Sophie stood still, shaking like a leaf. Carefully she went across to the door, gingerly trying the handle again. This time it opened. She quickly ran down the stairs. "Mum, mum, where are you?" She called out as she went into the kitchen.

Her mother came in from gardening, brushing the dirt from her trousers. She looked straight at Sophie, but somehow didn't seem to 'see her' – why? Sophie went across the kitchen and touched her mother's arm, but there was no response. She then saw her mother go out of the kitchen, up the stairs. "Sophie," she called, tapping gently on the bedroom door. Not receiving any reply, she carefully opened the door, but could see that the room was empty. Sophie's mobile phone lay on her bed. "She's gone out without it! She *never* does that! Maybe it will give me some hints as to where she has gone," thought her mother, picking the phone up, then putting it down on the bed again. "I need my glasses to see it!" She went downstairs again.

Meanwhile, Sophie had followed her mother upstairs. "Mum, mum!" she called, but however loudly she shouted, her mother could not see or hear her. At this moment, Sophie heard someone 'speaking' to her. The voice was asking her *why* she was always on her phone and *why* she insisted on using at every opportunity? The 'blue smoke' still seemed to waft over Sophie. She looked round desperately, but no-one was there. "Who..who are you?" she asked in a trembling voice.

"I am your phone!" was the reply. "You always want to use me even though your parents are trying to talk to you about different things. You insist on using me at the dinner table, which means no conversation takes place; this is rather rude, don't you think?"

Sophie bit her lip and nodded, but asked again, "Where am I?"

Her mobile phone explained that she had been 'swallowed up', so she could be taught a lesson to see things from a different point of view. "You *have* to see how annoying this is for your family and friends when they try to talk to you, but you're always talking to ME!"

Sophie looked puzzled, "I don't do I?"

"Yes you *do*, all the time, but I am going to try and help you spend less time with me. Ok?"

"How?" asked Sophie.

At this, her mobile phone said, "Just listen….."

"Where is she?" her mother was asking.

"Who was she talking to before she vanished?" asked dad.

"Who she's meeting up with is what's worrying me?" continued her mum. "Should we call the police?"

"She never speaks to us as she is always on her mobile phone. I think we are losing touch with her."

Sophie could hear the sadness in her parents' voices as all this was being discussed.

A tear ran down Sophie's face.

"Why won't she talk to us? We used to have such fun as a family!" Ruth turned to her husband, sobbing into his shoulder.

Her husband put his arm gently round her shoulders, "I think I *will* ring the police. She's never gone missing before and she hasn't taken her wretched phone this time!"

Sophie crumpled, "What can I do? I feel awful about this!"

Her mobile replied, "To start with you have to promise me you won't speak to me at meal-times, or when you're having a conversation with someone."

"How will that work?" Sophie queried.

"Oh, I will make sure your phone will not work at these valuable times. It will not matter how much you moan at me, or fiddle with my buttons, I will *not* release my hold," said her mobile.

"Do you reckon that will help me?" she asked.

Her mobile answered slowly, "Yes it will and it will work better with your help."

Sophie nodded, but she wasn't sure how, or if, it would change her habits. She had never seen using her mobile as a problem, but listening to her parents talking earlier, well, maybe, just maybe, she had been using it *far too much*. "Alright, what happens now? What do I have to do?" she asked.

Her mobile replied, "It's up to you to regulate your use of me. Use me to stay safe, don't contact people you do not know. Remember your friends and family want to talk face-to-face. I will be keeping an eye on you – good luck!" The 'blue smoke' faded..... Thoughtfully, she picked up her mobile, turning it over in her hand, it was not hot any longer.

She opened her bedroom door and went downstairs. "Hi mum!" Her mother turned round, a smile lighting up her face. "Sophie darling, where have you been? We couldn't find you in your room. Are you ok?" Her father put his arm round her and hugged her. She flung herself into her parents' arms.

"I'm so sorry. I heard you talking, but I couldn't reach out to you. I realise now just how awful I have been, using my phone all the time and not talking to you." Sophie continued, "From now on I'll only use my mobile when needed, promise!"

"Oh Sophie!" exclaimed her mother. "Your dad and I were so worried. We thought something had happened."

Sophie slowly replied, "My mobile has taught me a lesson," and she explained, as best she could.

Her father said, "Does that mean we will be able to talk together as a family again, sweetheart?"

"Yes, it's a promise!" she said as she hugged them both. Sophie felt something 'wriggle' in her pocket – mmm, was that her mobile phone giving her a gentle reminder of her promise?

Lightning Source UK Ltd.
Milton Keynes UK
UKOW06f0954010616

275386UK00001B/94/P